CURSED

Also by
BRUCE COVILLE

The Enchanted Files

CURSED

BRUCE COVILLE

illustrations by Paul Kidby

A Yearling Book

Text copyright © 2015 by Bruce Coville
Interior illustrations copyright © 2015 by Paul Kidby
Cover art copyright © 2016 by Andrew Bannecker

Yearling and the jumping horse design are registered trademarks of Penguin Random House LLC.

Visit us on the Web! randomhousekids.com

Educators and librarians, for a variety of teaching tools, visit us at RHTeachersLibrarians.com

Library of Congress Cataloging-in-Publication Data is available upon request.

ISBN 978-0-385-39250-1 (pbk.)

Printed in the United States of America
10 9 8 7 6 5 4
First Yearling Edition 2016

For Joe Monti—
Friend, mensch, inspiration

The Great Oath of the Brownies

(As sworn by every brownie when he or she comes of age to leave the Enchanted Realm and enter the human world)

We will maintain order and cleanliness in the households we inhabit, as is good and right.

For are we not brownies?

We will do a modest amount of mischief every day, mischief being an important part of a life well lived.

For are we not brownies?

We will avoid the eyes of all humans, and strive to be seen by none save the ones to whom we are bound.

For are we not brownies?

We will speak not of the Enchanted Realm to any human.

For are we not brownies?

And all this we swear, and all these things we will do, knowing that to break this oath is to risk fierce punishment.

For we are brownies, and subjects of the Queen of Shadows!

Saturday, September 19

I am about to embark on a great and fateful journey, and I am deep fretful. The thought of leaving Scotland fills me with woe.

To make things worse, I have just passed through a time of sorrow and loss.

Still, I am a brownie, fierce and proud, and should not be afraid.

Ach, I hope that is true! Oh, I know I am a brownie. And I know I am proud. But whether I am as fierce as I will need to be remains to be seen.

My cousin Fergus, who is the only other brownie left in our little highland village, has told me that when one is beset by fear and change, it can help to write about it.

That is why I have started this diary.

So far, it is not working.

Sunday, September 20

Last night when I told Fergus I thought the diary was of little use, he cried, "Ah, Angus, you don't understand. The diary is not just for calmin' yer frets. 'Tis also a way to save your memories!"

My memory is quite good all on its own, thank you very much. For example, I still remember the day over a hundred years ago when my da explained the curse that binds us to the McGonagalls.

You would think this would allow me some claim to wisdom. But Fergus said that as he is older than me by forty years, he is that much wiser, too. So I listen to his advice . . . unless he is offering it after he's had too much of that good nut ale he brews in the basement of the cottage he tends.

Those nights he spouts an awful stew of nonsense.

It occurs to me that even if this diary does not calm my frets, it may be wise to write down what happens. After all, I am about to undertake a journey into unknown territory. If I manage to survive, the tale may prove worth the telling. If it comes out well enough, I may even want to publish it someday!

With that in mind, I should probably write a bit about myself.

To start with, my name is Angus Cairns. I stand nearly a foot tall. I recently celebrated my 150th birthday, though you would not know it to look at me, as by human standards I appear to be less than a third that age. I have thick, curly brown hair (I am a brownie, after all!) and large green eyes. My nose is somewhat pointy, and my large ears are very pointy. I dress mostly in brown tunics with brown britches underneath. For a festive occasion, I sometimes add a red sash to liven things up. My shoes curl up a bit at the end, which is my one frivolity.

Also, I am extremely strong for my size. I hope this does not sound like a brag. It is simply a true thing about brownies.

We have to be strong in order to do all we must about a household!

Also, I have the gift of scurrying, which lets me move so fast when a human is near that I can appear to be but a blur to their eyes, so long as I begin before they sight me. I canna do this for great distances, of course. But in the moment it is quite useful.

As noted, I am long bound to the clan McGonagall. But—alas and woe!—my current McGonagall, Sarah, has grown old and ill. The thought of losing her pains me deeply. I have been the spirit of her house for many decades and tended it faithfully for all that time.

It is not often that a human and her brownie become friendly, but it happened in our case. This was due in part to a wicked trick Sarah played on me when she was young.

I will not speak more of that now, other than to note that I finally forgave her. In truth, I was delighted to discover she had mischief in her soul. Oh, the pranks we played when she was a lass . . . and even when she was what mortals call "old enough to know better."

Alas, one of the sorrows of being a brownie is that the humans in your life will never last as long as you do. Though I knew it was coming, it was still hard two nights ago when Sarah summoned me to her bedside to tell me the end was near.

Being not quite a foot tall, I climbed onto her nightstand, where I seated myself atop a pile of books. Once I was settled, she said softly, "Dearest Angus, I am not long for this world."

"I know, Sarah," I said. Then, to cheer her up, I added, "But you'll move on to a better one hereafter."

I envied her a bit in this. According to the priest in our small village, humanfolk have a soul that lives on after them, while we of the Enchanted Realm live on and on, but once gone, we're gone.

'Tis a sad thing to think on, so I prefer not to.

Besides, I believe the priest to be a moon-addled bampot.

"You know you're still bound to the McGonagall family, Angus. What you may not know is that none of this branch are left here in Scotland. And since the rule is that you must take service with the youngest female of age, I must send you to Alex Carhart, who lives across the sea in America."

I yelped at this. "Alex is a boy's name! You know 'tis to the youngest *female* of age that I must go!"

"Oh, Alex is a girl, all right. Her full name is Alexandra."

I crossed my arms and said, "Well, that's just silly. And I don't want to go. America is too far off. Not only that, from what we've seen on your television, 'tis a wild and barbaric place."

"Now, Angus! The Americans aren't barbaric. They're just ... different. And there's not much help for it, old friend. Gone I'll be, and that soon enough. So off to my great-great-great-niece you must go. As you well know, it is not a matter of choice but of the charge laid on both our families."

Which was true enough.

True or not, I was hardly happy about it. Nor would be any sensible brownie. To uproot myself and leave Scotland for the terrors of a new world? I'd rather peel off my clothes, roll in honey, and lie out in the sun where the ants could eat me. So though I dared not pitch a fit in front of Sarah, once I returned to my home beneath the stairs I had a prodigious one, with spirited cussing and much breaking of pottery and plates. (My own, of course, not Sarah's. That I would *NEVER* do.)

I always regret these fits afterwards. But when the

anger comes upon me, there is not much I can do. Generally, a fit will follow.

I cleaned it all up (of course!) and felt much dismay with myself for making such a mess to begin with. When I had all the shards and broken bits in a pile, I ran widdershins about them until I was going fast enough to make them disappear.

Now my shelves are bare.

Ah, weel. I couldn't have taken such things with me on my trip anyway. Too much to carry.

I have decided I should journey through the Enchanted Realm. It will be the fastest way for me to get to America, despite its dangers.

More concerning is the matter of the curse. It has been so long since it's been active that I am hoping it may have died away. After all, I have never been in a house where it was active. Even if not, perhaps it canna cross the great water?

That would be a blessing. Alas, I am fair sure the idea is naught but wishful thinking.

It would be best if this Alex Carhart I am assigned to has no brother or father about. Then I would not worry, for there would be none to suffer.

I wonder what she is like. I do hope she will be a tidy young thing, one who will appreciate a brownie and what he can do for her.

Monday, September 21

Dear Mr. and Mrs. Carhart,

Alex is a delightful girl, and I am glad to have her in my class.

That said, I have to tell you that her desk is the messiest I have seen in all my years of teaching.

I mean this quite literally. It <u>overflows</u> with paper and, well, stuff . . . some of it quite disgusting. Though Alex usually does her homework, it often takes five or ten minutes for her to locate it within the mess. That is, if she can find it at all! Though we are only three weeks into the school year, I already have a long list of missing work that Alex swears she has done but cannot locate.

Not handing in these assignments will have a serious impact on her grades for this quarter. To avoid further problems, here is a list of important upcoming due dates:

<u>Autobiography project:</u>
Due this Wednesday. Alex has had two weeks to work on it.

<u>Book report on novel of choice:</u>
Due Monday, Oct. 5

<u>Research report:</u>
Due Tuesday, Oct. 20

Could you <u>please</u> speak to her about this?
I am at my wit's end!

Sincerely,
Sheila Winterbotham

Location: bottom of Alex Carhart's backpack

Monday, September 21

When I went to talk to Sarah this morning, I said, "Do you think you could mail me to America? It might be safer that way."

She laughed, then coughed. Picking at the toast I had brought, she said, "Nae, 'tis a bad idea, Angus."

"And why is that?"

"Well, to begin with, what would you do for food and drink . . . not to mention what comes of eatin' and drinkin'?"

"I can hold my water a surprising amount of time," I replied primly.

Sarah laughed again, but it was dry and wispy. "And who's to package you up? I canna now do it myself, as you well know."

So we watched an old movie on her little TV. We mostly watch old Westerns, which is how I know America to be wild and barbarous.

Partway through the movie, Sarah fell asleep. Once she was making that little-old-lady snore of hers, a kind of blippitty-whistle, blippitty-whistle ('tis a sweet sound), I went belowstairs, where I spent a very distressing two hours trying to package myself up.

I will not write of the humiliating failure of this

attempt, save to say that packing tape and curly brown hair are not a good combination.

About the time I was recovering from another fit, I heard the front door open. It was Barbara-from-next-door, who comes in to check on Sarah every afternoon.

I heard her clomp up the stairs.

Barbara is a good woman, but she does clomp.

After about twenty minutes, I felt a pain in my heart and heard Barbara begin to wail. I did not need that sorrowful cry to know my Sarah was gone. I felt the bond between us snap in the very moment that she passed from this world. And so tomorrow and no later I must leave this house.

This all comes from Da carrying love messages for Ewan McGonagall all those years ago. Oh, Da! Why could you not have let well enough alone?

Ah, weel, that is all long past. The matter at hand is that I have but a fortnight to make it to America and my new human.

How I am to accomplish this journey, I do not know.

Last night I gathered what little I could carry—about half of my clothes, this diary, a spare hat, and my few bits of gold—and placed them in my pack.

Then I sealed it against wind and water.

So that they would not be found, I removed the rest of my belongings from the house, as is both custom and law for a brownie when the time for leaving comes. Most I took to Fergus. The documents that bind me, of course, I must carry in my pack.

I know so little of what is to come. Have any other brownies had to make this journey? Or are all my kind still safe here in Scotland?

I foresee a lonely time ahead.

Stop, Angus! Don't be maudlin. It does not befit a brownie.

Once all was in place, I sat and waited until sun was down and moon was up and the world grown soft and quiet. Then I walked slowly through the small tunnel I had dug so long ago, which brought me up beside the hedge behind Sarah's cottage. There I stood beneath a drooping fern to gaze back and remember.

I was taught that after his hundredth birthday, a

brownie should have no more need for tears. Still, I shed a few for my dear old Sarah.

For myself, too, I suppose, if I am to be honest.

When I could dally no longer, I went by secret ways to the place o' prayer. I didn't enter, of course. My kind are hardly welcome there. Instead I walked around it three times, widdershins. As I completed the third round, I slipped from the human world into the Enchanted Realm.

For those who do not know, I should state a thing or two about how the Realm works.

First, it is somehow connected to humans, for it is most rich and real where humans are . . . though not *too* many humans. For reasons I ken not, the Realm is weaker near cities, but strong near farms and villages.

Second, because the sea is not a place where humans live, there is not much of the Realm there. But the sea people—the merfolk, the selkies, and so on—have to have somewhere to be. As do the monsters of the deep. So there is indeed a sea within the Enchanted Realm, just not so broad and big as the one in the human world.

How this works, I do not know.

Anyway, my plan is to make my way to the edge of this Shadow Sea, then seek someone with wings to fly me to the other side. Alas, I have little to bargain with. I hope I will not have to make too great a promise in return for such a favor. It would be a binding contract, and I already have the binding of the curse to deal with.

So now I am heading for my new assignment.

I hope it will be a peaceful and congenial place. Even more, I hope that in time it will be a home, a genuine home, for that is what I most long for.

I also hope it will not have a cat.

HAPPY PETS VET

2929 Meadowbrook Road • New Glasgow, CT

September 23

Dear Mrs. Carhart,

We have taken a vote in the office, and I regret to inform you that we can no longer accept Bubbles as a patient.

In plain fact, the wound ratio after a visit from your cat is so high that three of my assistants have threatened to resign immediately if I allow "that bloodthirsty beast" (as they refer to Bubbles) back through our door.

I am attaching a photo of Geraldine's arm after our last encounter with Bubbles, in order to show you what I mean.

I do wish you the best of luck in finding another health-care provider for Bubbles. He is a fine specimen of cathood. May you have many happy years with him as your animal companion.

Very sincerely yours,

Elaine Coulter, DVM

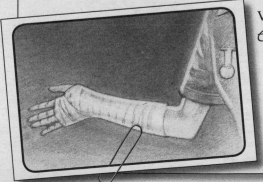

Feeling better today. I found a friendly toad—they grow large here in the Enchanted Realm—and he offered me a ride in return for three stories and a poem.

I take some pride in my storytelling and happily told him the story of why I am bound to the McGonagalls, as well as "Tam Lin" and "Thomas the Rhymer."

Toadback is not the most pleasant way to travel, as there is a lot of bounce and thump involved. Even so, it sped my journey greatly, which was good.

When we stopped for the day, I drew his portrait to remember him by.

He really was a fine figure of a toad, and it was a relief to have his help.

Time is pressing upon me. I have but nine days to reach my destination.

ABOUT THE

Encyclopedia
Enchantica

T he Encyclopedia Enchantica is the definitive guide to the people, places, and history of the Enchanted Realm.

All entries are written by established scholars of the Realm and provide clear and detailed information on every topic imaginable.

A copy of this essential book belongs in every home, castle, cottage, lair, tower, and residential cave of the Realm.

Order today!

—The editors

AUTOBIOGRAPHICAL ESSAY
by Alex Carhart

My name is Alex Carhart. I am eleven years old.

I was born in March. My father likes to say this was appropriate because I "came in like a lion."

(My father thinks he is very funny.)

I plan to be an artist when I grow up.

My family has always lived in the same house, and I am glad. I like being here. Also, if we had to move, I would have to clean up my room and pack my things, which would be a huge pain.

I love to read, but I am also athletic and like to play soccer.

I have long red hair, which I wear in braids most of the time. When I unbraid it and brush it out, my father says I am like a living sunset. He also says my hair is my crowning glory, which makes me proud.

I have an older brother named Bennett. He has red hair, just like me. Only he does not wear his hair in braids the way I do. We are both tired of being called gingers. It is "hairist" (that's a word I made up), and people should just stop.

Bennett likes to run, and he is a star in track and soccer. He is also a comic-book nerd. He has a huge collection of comics. I am not allowed to read any of them, or even touch them. He says that I mess them up. This makes me mad.

He calls me Al, which I kind of like and kind of hate, and sometimes Allie, which I don't mind.

I also have a little sister. Her name is Destiny. This is a family joke. My parents did not plan to have any children after me, which I think was smart, since one boy and one girl should be enough. According to my mother, Destiny "just happened."

Really.

She might as well say the stork brought her.

Anyway, my parents decided it was their fate to have a third child, and that is why they named her Destiny.

Personally, I am glad it happened. I love my little sister. She is in Kindergarten and she is very cute. Like me and Bennett, she has red hair. Everyone should get over it.

The most interesting thing about Destiny is that she has an imaginary friend named Herbert the Goblin. I think this is hilarious. My parents checked with a ~~psikiatrist~~ ~~psikiaterest~~ doctor, and he told them she is not crazy.

We were all happy to hear that.

My most memorable event was when we went to Disney World and Bennett threw up on Space Mountain. He still gets mad if I talk about that. I guess I'm not supposed to think it was funny. But I do.

My mother is a supervisor at Happy Oaks Senior Home. I think she likes her job, but I also know it makes her sad sometimes. That is because after someone comes to live at Happy Oaks, his or her next move is usually in a big wooden box.

Mom says that her worst patients are the ones who got more sour as they got older, and her best are the ones who somehow love life no matter how old and tired they might be. Her very favorite patient is the oldest one in the home, so old that no one really knows her age because her papers are kind of a mess. Mom calls this woman her happy mystery.

My father is a CPA. That's Certified Public Accountant, which most people think means he is a "numbers guy" and dull and dry. This is not true. Dad likes to write songs with his friend Pete. Dad does the music and Pete does the words. Some of their songs are pretty good, especially the one about two octopuses trying to learn to waltz. That one always makes me laugh.

I think Dad secretly wishes he was a musician instead of a CPA.

I think that would be cool.

That is my family, and that is my life. I think it is pretty good, and I am happy to be me.

THE END

PS: I would have typed this, but Bennett was hogging the computer.

9/26

Alex—

This is quite good, if a bit short. Your family sounds lovely.

Unfortunately, I had to deduct several points because this was two days late.

I also deducted five points because of the ketchup stain. (At least, I hope it was ketchup!)

—Mrs. W

Saturday, September 26

I have been three days by the edge of the sea and have yet to find a winged creature who will fly me to the other side. Wretched flibbertigibbets! It's not only their wings that have feathers. I'm convinced their heads are stuffed with 'em, too.

If only I could say, "Ah, weel. As none will take me across, I must stay here instead." Alas, that I cannot do. With each day that passes, an ache grows within me, as if some foul worm were a'gnawin' at my guts. I know it is nae a worm, of course. It's the queen's curse eatin' at me. Yearn as I might to stay in Scotland, I must cross the water and find my way to my new charge.

Encyclopedia Enchantica

SELKIE

The selkie folk live in the cold northern waters around the isles of Great Britain. They have two forms. In the sea, they are as seals and move swiftly and smoothly through the water in their sleek, furry bodies. But when

they come to land, they shed this skin to reveal their human form, which is generally quite beautiful.

Should someone capture the skin of a selkie, the creature is then in his or her captor's power, and many the tale is told of a female selkie forced to marry a human man. Some of these marriages are happy, some not, but always there is a part of the selkie's heart that longs to return to the water and once more be a seal in the sea.

A human woman may summon a male selkie by shedding seven tears into the sea at high tide. Though these sea-men tend to be very handsome, generally such meetings do not end well.

—Abelard Chronicus, Gnome

I have my way across! It is not the way I would have chosen, but desperation will drive a brownie to do strange things. Yestereve at the shore I spied one of the selkie folk. She had shed her sealskin and was lounging about in her human altogether. This would have shocked me at one time, but you can't live over 150 years and still be startled by such things.

Happily, discovering her in this state gave me all I needed to gain her help, for while she was combing out her hair, I went to the water's edge and hauled her sealskin into the woods.

Then I sat beneath a tree and waited.

When the selkie lass was ready to return to the water, she went to slip into her skin. Oh, what a wailing she unleashed when she found she could not find it!

At the sound of her woe, I came skipping down the beach, all syrup and innocence. Eyes wide, I said, "Why, what's wrong, miss?"

"Oh, brownie!" she cried. "Someone has stolen my skin, and I cannot return to the sea without it."

"Nae, it has not been stolen," I tell her. "Merely hidden, and glad I'll be to return it in exchange for a wee favor."

"And what favor would that be?" she asked, glaring at me.

"I need passage to the other side of the Shadow Sea."

Her glare grew fiercer. "That's a mighty high price, little man."

This was not a good thing to say to me.

"I am nae a man!" I cried, and the fit was upon me. "I am a brownie, as you well know. A brownie, a brownie, not some stinking human with great clumping feet and eyes that do not see. I am a brownie fierce and proud, you silly, soggy, seagoing wicked wench of wetness. And I still know where your skin is, which you do not!"

I was leaping up and down now, shaking my tiny fists at her. Though she was many times taller than me, I think I frightened her.

"All right, brownie," she said with a sigh. "I'll do as you ask."

I have done many foolish things in my time, but I am nae fool enough to take a mere promise from a selkie. I made her cup water from the waves into her hands, then swear by the sea itself that she would deliver me safe and do me no harm.

She grumbled, but did as I asked. When she had completed the oath, I fetched her skin.

We depart in the morning.

9/28

Dear Mr. and Mrs. Carhart,

Destiny is a charming child. However, I have a growing concern regarding her persistence in talking about her imaginary friend.

Please do not misunderstand me. Imaginary friends are all well and good, and many children have them. But by first grade most children have learned to separate the imaginary from the real, and don't insist that their imaginary friends require a seat right next to them. This insistence on fantasy strikes me as unhealthy.

Unhealthy or not, it is definitely disruptive. Can you imagine what it would be like if I had to provide two chairs for every child in my class, as I currently must do for Destiny and her "friend"? We would hardly be able to move across the room!

I implore you to try to convince Destiny that "Herbert the Goblin" needs to stay home. Perhaps you can invent some tasks or chores the creature needs to perform while Destiny is at school.

Also, you might consider counseling.

I am quite fond of Destiny, but I do worry about her.

Sincerely,

Ms. Lorna Kincaid

If I never again see the sea, it will be fine with me. The last two days were among the most wretched of my life.

Why did nobody tell me you canna drink seawater?

Nor did I have any idea how horrible it is to be seasick. I spent most of the trip lying on my back atop that selkie's head, groaning and wishing I could die. I got no sympathy from her, of course. She said it served me right for tricking her.

And then there were the mermaids. You'd think they had never seen a brownie riding a selkie before. All right, they probably hadn't. Even so, that's no excuse for the way they circled around us, singing nasty songs accusing the selkie of being in love with me. And other songs even more insulting than that. The one that made me maddest was:

Selkie and brownie,
Swimming cross the seas.
Watch out, selkie—
Brownie has fleas!

I felt the urge to pitch a fit, but the top of a selkie's head in the middle of the sea is no place for such a thing. For certain it was a wise move when I made the selkie take the oath to carry me safe across. The mermaids upset her so much, I am certain she was tempted to dive deep and stay under till I was fit for naught but fish food.

And there are some mighty strange fish swimming in the Shadow Sea!

When we finally reached the far shore and the selkie dropped me off, she said, "Well, that's done, brownie. I'll be back to my own life, and hoping I never have the grievous misfortune to see you again, *little man*."

I again felt the urge to pitch a fit, though I knew she had said it to taunt me. Just as well I had not the energy for it. I realize now she would have been happy to see me lose my temper.

Still, 'tis a sad state of affairs when I am too tired to tell off a selkie.

My travels are nae over. I still have to make my way to this Alex Carhart. Finding her is not much of a problem, as I am drawn to her by the queen's curse. It's as if I am a fish pulled by a hook.

But who knows what I will find when I am pulled into the boat?

I do wish Sarah could have let this Alex know I was coming. I wonder how she will react when she discovers I am to stay with her as long as she lives!

Maybe I won't tell her.

Yes, I think that's best. Though Sarah and I became

friends, the curse does not require me to get to know the person I am bound to. I will simply clean and tidy for her in secret.

No need to become friends. One human friend was enough.

They only go and get old on you.

Encyclopedia Enchantica

THE ENCHANTED REALM ON OTHER CONTINENTS

Though this encyclopedia focuses on the Realm as it manifests in Europe and the British Isles, it is important to acknowledge that it exists around the world. That is why there are separate volumes for each of the continents (though the one for Antarctica is quite slim). We should also note that the folk of the Enchanted Realm of the various continents were in contact long before the humans of those places managed to find each other. This can be explained by two factors: the great elven ships, and the explorations of such creatures as the Pegasi, the Griffins, and the Greater Dragons.

The woods of the Enchanted Realm in America are different from those I knew in Scotland. Different, but not unpleasant. Oak, ash, and beech still abound, which is comforting.

I made good progress today. The curse has kept me very agitated, but the closer I get to where I belong, the more it seems to settle. So I was actually able to enjoy the walk for the first time since I set out.

On the other hand, the closer I get, the more I fret about what I will find when I arrive.

It will be a relief to reach the end of my journey and return to my true work of keeping things neat and tidy.

To: My Fabulous Students

From: Mrs. Winterbotham

Subject: JOURNALS

Date: Friday, October 2

Dear Writers,

    As discussed in class today, next week we will begin keeping journals. This is a special assignment, something that you will be doing more for yourselves than for me. I am never going to read them. *I promise!* These are just for you!!

    Why do I say "journal" rather than "diary"? Here's one way to look at it: A diary is about what you do, a journal is about what you *think*! About what you want to work on in your life. About figuring out who you are. A diary tells us what you did. A journal discusses who you will *become*!

    This is how it will work: Three times a week (M/W/F), we will take class time to work on our journals. I say "we" because I will be journaling right along with you! I will *not* be working on lesson plans or correcting papers. I will be doing the same thing you are.

    I feel this is the best way to show you how seriously I take this.

Your assignment for this weekend is to find a blank book of some kind to serve as your journal. Please have it in class for Monday.

I call this project a lifesaver . . . you are saving something of yourself FOR yourself!

Remember the proverb: "The shortest pencil beats the longest memory." I *guarantee* that the day will come when the YOU you are to become will be delighted to have this.

—Mrs. W

Friday, October 2

Today as I was scrambling over a rock formation, a person suddenly loomed before me. He was a giant as compared to me, yet no more than waist-high to an adult human. His skin had a coppery cast, and his long hair was midnight black. He wore blue pants. His white shirt was bright with beadwork, done in patterns new to me.

Why did it never occur to me that there would be people native to the Enchanted Realm on these strange shores?

"Well, little man," he said. "Why are you crossing my lands?"

"I am nae a little man!" I cried, on the edge of a fit. I managed to pull myself back. Unlike the selkie, it was possible this . . . person did not know a brownie when he saw one. I was now on the far side of the sea, after all.

"Then what are you?" asked the big fellow as he bent to look at me more closely. "I have never seen your like."

I did not like being examined like this, and it pushed me into crankiness. "I am a brownie," I snapped. "It's plain as day, and if ye canna see it, then you need new eyes!"

The wretched fellow laughed at me! "And do you know what I am?" he asked.

"Now how should I know that?" I asked angrily.

"Well, how should I know what you are?"

That stopped me in my tracks.

"That's quite a temper you have, brownie," the fellow said.

I hung my head. Though I am by nature as sweet as dew on a rose petal, my temper is my downfall. And here I was, in this new land, meeting my first new person, and already acting the pepperpot.

"So, you're a brownie," said my new acquaintance. "I've heard of your kind, but never met one. A long way from home, aren't you?"

"A very long way."

"Have you come to steal our land?"

I looked at him in puzzlement. He smiled, showing admirably white teeth. "Just a joke. A lot of land stealing went on here in the past, so we ask that question of any newcomer."

"And who is this 'we' you speak of?" I asked.

"I am one of the Makiaweesug."

"And what might be the Makiaweesug?"

"We're people of the Enchanted Realm, just as you. We have been here since time out of mind."

"And how do you know I'm of the Realm?"

"Well, there's your size, to begin with. But mostly there's the fact that you are here in the Realm to begin with."

This made me feel a right fool. Drawing myself up to

my full not quite twelve inches, I said, "Though I am of the Realm, I am just passing through. I've been assigned to a lass who lives not far, and I am bound by ancient pact to her family."

"Ancient pact" is not quite true, of course, as it is not an agreement that ties me to the McGonagalls but a curse. But I do not like to speak of that.

"And how do you know where to find this girl?"

"I canna help but find her, for I am drawn as a moth to the flame, a fish to the worm, or a needle to a lodestone."

"Rather fond of words, aren't you?" said the Makia-weesug.

I paused for a moment, then said, "Yes."

This short answer earned me a smile and his name, which turned out to be Weegun.

Weegun

Note long hair

Me, slightly embarrassed

Nice boots!
I rather envy them.

No toe curl, though

ANGUS

When someone of the Enchanted Realm tells you his name, it is only fit and right that you should do the same, so I bowed and said, "I am Angus Cairns."

"Well, Angus Cairns, would you like me to walk a while with you?"

It was a pleasant offer, and Weegun seemed a good-hearted fellow. Or perhaps he just wanted to make sure I wasn't up to any mischief. Either way, I did not think I could refuse him. "I would be glad of your company," I said, which was hardly a lie at all.

So on we walked. As we did, Weegun told me about his people. Unlike we brownies, they have as little to do with the human world as they can.

My new friend also named for me the trees and flowers that I did not know. I began to feel quite glad that I had met him.

We had been going a bit when I said, "The pull on my heart grows suddenly stronger. I think we draw near my new home."

"Then I will leave you here, Angus Cairns. We are close to the edge of the Realm, and my people do not leave it unless we must."

I thanked him for his company, and he wished me well.

Soon after, I came to a place of mists and knew I was about to return to the human world. I decided to write this before I did. Who knows what I will find on the other side? Perhaps this will be the last time I ever make an entry in this diary.

Besides, I must wait until dusk, for I must not be seen.

LATER

I just read over what I have written, and realized I do not need to put down who said what so often. It was clear to me when I was talking and when Weegun was talking.

That's good writing, I think.

This will save me a lot of time and ink.

Also, it's neater.

10/2

Dear Ms. Kincaid—
    Thank you for telling us your concerns regarding Destiny. Her father and I had a little talk with her this evening, and I am happy to report that the situation regarding "Herbert the Goblin" seems to have resolved itself. To be specific, according to Destiny, "Herbert left because he had to go back to work."
    She did cry about this a little.
    I hope this change will make the classroom situation easier. We appreciate your concerns for our child.

                Sincerely,
                Ellen Carhart

Saturday, October 3

I have reached my goal.

More than that I cannot bring myself to write just now. I need another day to recover not only from the terrors of the journey but also from the shock of what I found when it was over.

For now, I will say only that I can see it was fate that brought me here. Bringing order to this place will not be merely a task.

It will be a sacred mission.

From: A-Car@kid2kid.com
To: T-Jenks@kid2kid.com
Date: 10/3
Subject: My Room

Tiana—

AAAAAAAARGH!

My mother is driving me crazy! She keeps yelling at me to clean up my room.

I hate wasting time cleaning. It's stupid.

BESIDES, I LIKE MY ROOM JUST THE WAY IT IS!

Wanna swap moms?
Alex

PS: I measured today and my braids are almost down to my butt! Another few months and I'll achieve my goal of being able to sit on them.

PPS: I am looking forward to using the knots in the ends of my braids to bonk boys on the head!

Sunday, October 4

I think I have recovered from my frights enough to write down what I have done and what I have seen.

By the way, Cousin Fergus was right after all. Keeping this diary does help. If I were not writing these things down, they would be exploding inside me.

Back to where I left off . . .

Once dusk fell and I left the Enchanted Realm, I found myself at the edge of a forest, with no idea how much farther I had to travel. I hoped it was not far. Being out in the open at night is dangerous for one of my size. My greatest fear, of course, was of being taken by an owl. That goes back to Da's adventure 300 years ago . . . which is why I am in this situation to begin with.

As it turned out, owls were the least of my problems. The great danger came from the human roads. Och, never have I seen such roads! Great rivers of stone, with cars and trucks barreling along as if their arses were on fire!

I waited for hours at the edge of the first road. Well, I stood at the edge for a bit, then drew back and lurked in the bushes, because the noise and the wind caused by all that metal hurtling by were like to drive me mad.

As the night grew late and the road grew calmer, I

finally had a chance to cross the wretched thing, dodging only one truck as it raced towards me.

My ability to scurry came in handy here and likely saved my life.

I had to cross several more roads before the night was out. Fortunately, none was as wide and horrifying as the first.

After an hour or so, I came to a collection of houses. I felt myself pulled irresistibly towards one of them.

I had reached my new home at last!

At that realization, I was struck by a greater pang than I had expected. It is a sad thing to come home after a long journey and have no one there to welcome you. It is even worse to have no one know that you've come home at all!

Well, let that be. The first problem now was how to get inside, something I hadn't had to worry about in more than half a century. I circled the place, looking for a door into the cellar. To my surprise, there was none.

I did not worry, for it was a brick home and therefore easy to climb, since bricks are almost as good as stepping stones for my small hands and feet. Without much effort I scrambled up the wall to a windowsill. But when I climbed over the edge, I found that the window was sealed tight.

No matter, thought I, I'll just move on to the next. Ha! I circled all the way around the wretched place without finding a single window open by so much as a crack.

What do these Americans do for fresh air?

I climbed to the next level and found the same problem. The only bit of progress here was that as I made my way around the house (clinging to the wall some fifteen feet above the ground, a vast distance for one of my size), I found the room that my heart told me belonged to Alex.

Not that it made much difference. Her windows were shut as tight as all the others.

Filled with despair, I returned to the ground. Circling the house once more, I was surprised to discover a flap in the back door! It was only about a foot high, and so easy to push up that I had to wonder if they had been expecting me. No, that couldn't be possible. But what kind of thinking is it to seal a house so tightly, then put in a flap that would give entrance to any small wild thing that pushed against it?

I can write no more. My hand trembles with horror as I think of what happened next.

From: Swinterbotham@edu.ctx.net
To: Familycarhart@br-net.com
Date: 10/4
Subject: Missing Assignments

Dear Mr. and Mrs. Carhart—

Did you receive my previous note regarding Alex's
work and her desk? I have been awaiting a response.

Sincerely,
Sheila Winterbotham

From: Swinterbotham@edu.ctx.net
To: Familycarhart@br-net.com
Date: 10/4
Subject: Missing Assignments

MESSAGE REJECTED. MAILBOX FULL.

I've had time to settle, and I think I can finish now.

So . . . when I went through the flap, I found myself in the kitchen. But I scarce had a chance to catch my bearings before I heard a sound behind me, and then a questioning "Meow?"

I turned in time to see a CAT come pushing through the flap. That was when I finally realized the true purpose of that insane contraption: to let the CAT go in and out at will!

And this was not just any cat. It was a huge and nasty brute with thick orange fur and the devil in its eyes.

That I am not resting in its stomach even now is mostly due to the fact that it was outside when I came through the flap myself.

What manner of people are these that I've been sent to live with, who keep a monster as a pet and give the thing free access to the outside world so it can prey on any wee creature that takes its fancy? I shudder to think how many poor little birds have uttered their last note—not a sweet song, nae, but a strangled squawk—as a result of a fur-faced, carrot-colored demon being free to use this devil's doorway as it pleases.

I cannot help but ask myself anew why, oh why, did Da see it his duty to help Ewan McGonagall all those years ago?

When the monster (which is to say, the CAT) spotted me, I thought all was lost. If I could not escape, I might fare no better than the helpless, blood-drenched songbirds I was sure had perished in those slavering jaws. The beast crouched into a hunting pose and its tail twitched in a way I knew all too well. It had murder on its mind and a taste for blood on its tongue!

I took my pack from my back.

The beast sprang!

I swung my pack and smacked it square on the nose.

It let out the most horrid yowl and leaped back. In that moment, I was able to bound away. The fiend recovered, then sprang again. But I had time to scurry behind the refrigerator (which is twice the size of the one my Sarah had in her little kitchen).

To my disgust, the backside of the coldbox was thick with dust and grime! Just thinking of it makes me want to leap into a tub and scrub myself clean!

The cat crouched outside my hiding place. I could see one burning eye, like a lamp from the pits of hell. A huge paw reached into my filthy place of refuge, trying to snag me with its daggerlike claws. I shrank back just far enough to avoid those deadly hooks.

The beast stayed there for what seemed like ten years,

though that could not have been the case, since the sun had not yet risen when my nemesis finally got bored and went back out through Satan's Flap (as I now think of that hole in the door).

I waited until I was sure it would not return. Then, grateful that the family had yet to wake, I made my way up the stairs. Climbing stairs is an effort for me because of my size. But these stairs were easier than the ones I was used to, as they were covered with a thick blue carpet I could wedge my fingers into to pull myself up.

The upper floor had four bedrooms. I already knew which was Alex's, as I have an excellent sense of direction even after being chased by a slavering beast, then going round a twist in a stairway. Of course, even lacking that I would have been drawn to her room by the binding of the curse.

Alex's door was not closed, so I was able to enter easily. My first piece of good luck that long, hard night!

The floor was cluttered. This made me twitch, but there was no point in starting to tidy up right then. I was too exhausted.

I needed a place to sleep, so I went to the closet. The door was not closed tight, but when I pulled it open by another few inches, my heart sank within me.

I was faced with a wall of clutter!

What kind of mastermind of messiness was this child to whom I had been assigned?

I climbed the Clutter Wall. I found the top of the mess about three feet above the floor. Rumpled clothes and a couple of empty shoe boxes covered the surface. Three garments actually hung from hangers. I climbed one of these easily enough, got my hands on the rod that went from wall to wall, and was able to grab hold of the shelf. I swung a leg over and scrambled onto it, blessing the great strength that is my birthright. Once there I pushed a few things around to make room enough to hide a shoe box. Then I returned to the lower level and, with some effort, dragged one up. Then I slept.

Had nightmares.

FROM THE JOURNAL OF
ALEX CARHART

10/4 (Sun.)

Mom bought me this journal for Mrs. Winterbotham's crazy new assignment. I decided to practice writing in it before Monday. But I don't know what the point is. It's not like anything interesting ever happens to me. Of course, Mrs. W said our journals are more for writing about what we think and feel than what we do.

She also promised she would never read them.

I wonder if that is true.

Okay, here is one thing I think. I think our teacher has a strange name. Winterbotham. What kind of name is that? It makes me think she must have a cold butt.

I wonder if she sits on ice cubes when she goes home.

Wow. I can't believe I just wrote that down. This journal keeping could be dangerous.

I guess I'll find out pretty soon if Mrs. W was telling the truth when she said she wouldn't read these!

(Mrs. Winterbotham, if you are reading this, I am sorry I made fun of your name. But of course you can't tell me if you accepted my apology or not.)

Since I'm on the subject, here are some other things about my teacher:

1. Her name makes her sound older than she is.

2. Her husband is a hottie. (He rides a motorcycle!)

3. She has the world's best handwriting.

4. If she would just stop busting me about my desk, I would really like her.

I am now faced with the most daunting task of my life. Where to begin?

With the evidence of my own eyes, I suppose. This room is a disaster, a catastrophe, a sty, a horror, and an abomination.

I am sure there must be more words, but I canna think of them right now.

There is STUFF everywhere, on every surface. Where does someone even get hold of so much stuff . . . especially someone so young?

Here is a partial list, to offer proof I am not shamming:

Papers
Papers, wadded up
Books
Pencils
Half pencils
Broken pencils
Pencil shavings
Bits of string
Globs of modeling clay
Tubes of paint
Clothes, clean

Clothes, dirty
Clothes, filthy
Clothes, fit only for burning
A half glass of orange juice
Three dead flies, floating in orange juice
Food (many kinds)
Moldy food
Food likely to kill anyone who tastes it

Cleaning this up will be hard, very hard. But the thought of how happy my new human will be when she sees what I have done gives me the strength to go on.

Monday, October 5 (evening)

I have never been so insulted in my life!

I doubt any brownie has ever suffered such mortification.

When this creature, this ... this *human* came into her room after school today, was she delighted to discover it clean and tidy? (Well, partially clean and tidy. There's much more still to do. Even so, I made enough of a start that it looks like a different room. For one thing, you can actually see several square feet of floor!)

Was she thankful for the enormous amount of work I had done?

HA!

I repeat: HA!

Instead of exclaiming in delight, the wretched girl let out a screech worthy of a banshee.

"Aaaaaaah!" she cried. "Who did this?"

Then she called the police.

TRANSCRIPT OF CALL FROM ALEX CARHART (AC) TO POLICE DISPATCHER (PD) REGARDING INTRUDER IN HER ROOM:

AC: Hello, police? I need to report a prowler.

PD: (alarmed) Is he on the premises? Are you in any danger? Do you want me to dispatch a squad car?

AC: No, I don't think he's here now. But whoever it was snuck into my room and cleaned it!

PD: <laughter> I'm sure it was your mother, dear.

AC: NO! My mother swore she would never set foot in my room again until I had cleaned it up myself.

PD: Well, mothers can be strange, dear.

AC: Stop calling me dear! This is an emergency. I have some weird creeper sneaking into my room and organizing my stuff.

PD: Well, if you get tired of him—or her—send the perp in my direction. I could use someone like that.

AC: You're laughing at me!

PD: No, no. Just jealous.

AC: So you're not going to help me? Thanks for nothing!

By the time Alex was off the phone, two young people were standing at her door.

One was a tall, redheaded lad—quite handsome except for the way that he slouched.

I despair of the posture of modern youth.

The other was a wee girl who looked to be no more than five or six. She was clutching a doll. Her long hair, also red, fell nearly to her waist.

"Alex, what the heck is wrong with you?" asked the boy.

"Look around!" she shouted in response.

"Hey, I can see your floor!"

"Very funny!"

"I think it looks nice," said the little girl.

It was good to know there is one sensible person in this family! Alas, Alex's response was to growl, "I liked it the way it was!"

"Then why did you clean it up?" asked the big brother. "Did Mom finally lower the boom?"

"I didn't clean it up! Didn't you hear what I just said to the police? Some creeper sneaked in here and cleaned my room while I wasn't looking!"

The big brother smirked. "Okay, I got it. You cleaned

it up but don't want to admit it. Now you want us to forget it."

With that rhyme, I felt my stomach clench. Was the curse I am supposedly doomed to carry with me taking effect? I felt sick at the thought.

"Maybe you have a magical friend, like Herbert," said the little girl.

Big brother rolled his eyes at this, but it made me wonder if someone else from the Enchanted Realm is living in this house. Little as I like it here, lonely as I am, I'm not sure how I would feel about sharing the place with another magical being.

Just then we heard an unholy howling. A chill ran down my spine at the sound. Then I realized it was what they call a siren, as I've seen in the old movies I watched with Sarah.

Next came a knocking at the door.

All three children ran down the stairs. Oh, how I longed to run after them to see what was going on. I could not, of course, as I'm nae to be seen, except possibly by Alex, though right now I canna think of any reason I would want that to happen.

I learned soon enough what it was all about. That was because when Mrs. Carhart returned home, she came to Alex's door and, with enough ice in her voice to freeze a small pond, said, "Did you really call the police today?"

The girl is made of sterner stuff than I thought, for she rose from her desk and said, "I certainly did!"

"Why?" asked the mother.

"Because you didn't warn me that you hired someone to clean my room. I thought it had been done by some creepy prowler."

Mrs. Carhart actually snorted, which was not very ladylike. Then she said, "The day we can afford a housekeeper, he or she takes on my work first!"

"Well, then who did . . . this?" sputtered the girl, waving her arm to indicate the beautiful tidiness I had imposed on the horrible clutter.

Mrs. Carhart rolled her eyes. "Look, Alex, I understand you take some perverse pride in having your room look like it's inhabited by apes. I also assume that my threat to ground you for a million years has had some effect. But you can't go calling the police just to create an excuse for having cleaned your room."

"I did *not* clean my room!" cried Miss Alex, as if denying that she had just committed an ax murder.

Mrs. Carhart sighed. "You are the strangest child," she said. Then she turned and walked away, muttering something about bigger problems in her life.

Alex returned to her desk. Growling savagely, she rammed a long metal tool through the chest of the clay man she had been working on.

I must admit, I flinched at that.

The girl seems infuriated by the idea of anyone thinking she cleaned the room herself and clearly takes an inexplicable delight in her messiness.

I fear she may consider it a mark of her "artistic temperament."

My only hope is that when she begins to understand the joy of having a constantly clean room, she will change her mind.

Tuesday, October 6

Today while Alex was away at school, I continued my efforts to wrest order out of the chaos. By the time she arrived home, the clothes she had left strewn about the floor had been tended to . . . most put in her hamper, which she does not seem to know how to use. Also the bits of clay she had left here and there had been gathered into a tidy ball and placed in the center of her desk.

The cat—curse the furry hide of the beast!—was lying on her bed, purring contentedly, as if it thought I had cleaned up this mess just for its benefit!

When Alex saw how pristine her room was, she looked at the cat and said, "Did you do this, Bubbles?"

Bubbles?

BUBBLES?!?

By the Queen and all her court, what kind of name is Bubbles for a creature like this? Lucifer or Bloodclaw Reddifang would be more appropriate.

As if the name of the cat was not bad enough, what Alex did next struck horror in my heart. She turned her back-pack upside down over her bed! Out poured an appalling jumble of books, pens and pencils in various stages of usefulness, candy wrappers, rubber bands, sparkly bits of rocks, three crayons stuck together, an empty bag that once held some salty snack food, four used tissues, and several crumpled sheets of paper.

"Bubbles" hissed, then bounded off the bed and out of the room.

Even savage beasts are offended by the girl's slovenliness!

With the foul creature gone, I couldn't help myself. As soon as Alex went to her desk and started to fiddle with her clay, I darted out of the closet and went to work. I unstuck crayons, lined up pencils, and tossed trash from the bed into the wastebasket, all in perfect silence. Also, I uncrumpled the papers.

I was surprised to find she has very neat handwriting.

I wasn't worried about her catching me. If you observe humans closely for over a hundred years and pay attention to what they do, it's not hard to guess a movement before they make it. So it was no problem to scurry off the bed and be under it before she even turned around.

What *WAS* a problem was her shriek of "What is going on here?"

I felt a pinch in my heart at that. All I want is to do a good job and be appreciated a bit. But it seems that may be impossible with this girl.

Heart aching, I waited until she left the room, then returned to my closet hiding space.

Wednesday

Dear Mrs. Winterbotham,

    Here is my book report that was due on Monday.

    I am sorry it is late.

    I am also sorry it is crumpled and has a stain on it.

    I actually had it in my backpack to give to you on Monday, but it got buried under some other stuff and I couldn't find it. And then I looked all over at home that night. But it wasn't there, of course, because it was still in my backpack. I found it yesterday afternoon.

          Your favorite student (I hope!),

          Alex Carhart

Today I went out of Alex's room with two thoughts in mind. One, to explore the house. Two, to do a bit of mischief.

I could do this freely because the cat, being like all cats lazy at heart, was sleeping soundly. I knew this for a fact because the insolent thing was curled up on Alex's bed.

Here are the things I discovered:

The brother is neater than Alex. That said, his athletic shoes have a smell that would fell a lesser brownie. Also, he has a large collection of magazines with oddly costumed characters on the front. I opened one. The characters all spoke in bubbles coming out of their heads. Very strange.

The little sister has many stuffed toys. She seems especially fond of unicorns. I braided the mane of one of them as a wee bit of mischief.

Also to show my disapproval of unicorns with pink manes.

The remaining room on this floor I have heard Mrs. Carhart call the guest bedroom.

All I can say is a guest would have a hard time sleeping in it, given the mountain of stuff piled on the bed.

There is also a bathroom, but I have seen that already, as it is where I have been doing my personal business.

Downstairs is the kitchen, of course. They have a machine that washes dishes! How Sarah would have loved that.

There is also a dining room and a living room, which has a machine with an enormous screen. It looks like a television, but it is hard for me to imagine a television could be that big. If it really is a television, it must be terrifying to watch. You would feel like the horses were going to run right over you!

Finally there is Mr. and Mrs. Carhart's room. Attached to it is the biggest bathroom I have ever seen! Their bedroom is not a sty like Alex's, but it is no model of neatness, either. They hardly set a good example for the child.

I could not get into the cellar, for the door was shut tight.

Though it is to Alex I am bound, it is her household that I am to care for. After Sarah's tiny cottage, this place is overwhelming.

Truly, it is a lot for one small brownie.

First Floor

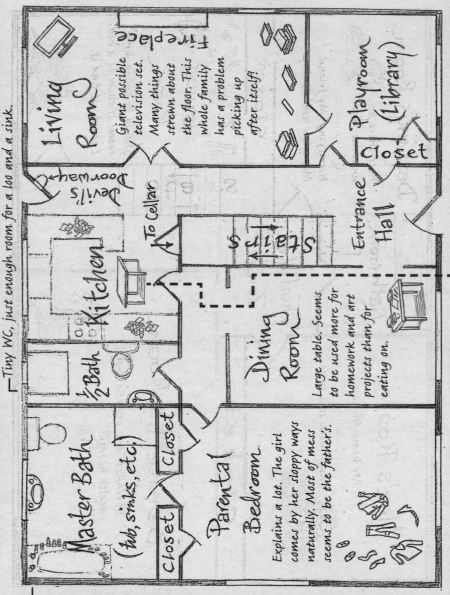

Tiny WC, just enough room for a loo and a sink.

Living Room

Giant possible television set. Many things strewn about the floor. This whole family has a problem picking up after itself!

Devil's Doorway

To cellar

Kitchen

½ Bath

Master Bath

(tub, sinks, etc.)

Closet

Closet

Parental Bedroom

Explains a lot. The girl comes by her sloppy ways naturally. Most of mess seems to be the father's.

Dining Room

Large table. Seems to be used more for homework and art projects than for eating on.

STAIRS

Entrance Hall

Playroom (Library)

Closet

Biggest bathroom I have ever seen! Also, six kinds of shampoo and seven kinds of soap. Why does anyone need more than one bar of soap? I do not understand.

Second Floor

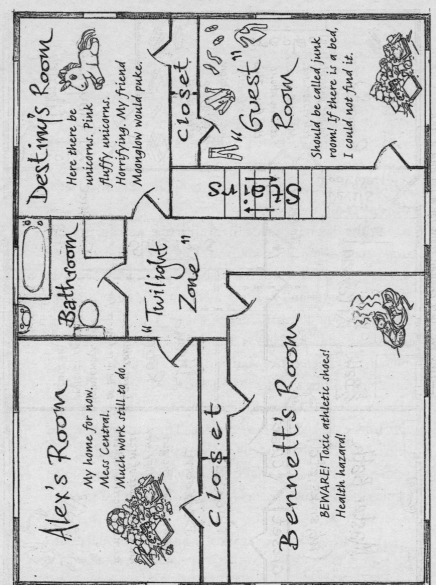

Destiny's Room
Here there be unicorns. Pink fluffy unicorns. Horrifying. My friend Moonglow would puke.

Closet

"Guest" Room
Should be called junk room! If there is a bed, I could not find it.

Stairs

Bathroom

"Twilight Zone"

Alex's Room
My home for now. Mess Central. Much work still to do.

Closet

Bennett's Room
BEWARE! Toxic athletic shoes! Health hazard!

Kitchen: Nice room. Lots of equipment. There doesn't seem to be much cooking going on, though. Big table. Also many bags of dry foods. I sampled some. Most either too salty or too sweet. Blech.

Today the wicked girl got the better of me. Ah, weel. At least things are out in the open now.

The afternoon started much as it had yesterday, with young Miss Mess coming into her room and once again dumping her backpack upon the bed. Such disorder! Such disrespect for my efforts!

As the day before, I waited until she was busy at her desk, then climbed down from the closet and scurried across the floor. I scaled the bedspread and went to work, moving silently and keeping alert for any signs that she might be about to turn around.

A few minutes later, I caught a hint of movement. Blessing my keen ears, I scurried under the bed.

Being willing to enter the pit of chaos that waited below should be taken as a measure of my desire not to be seen. Oh, under the bed is a horrid place! The dust, all clumped and nasty! The abandoned toys, broken and crippled! The scatter of little plastic bricks, mismatched socks, crumpled papers, used tissues, broken crayons! 'Tis enough to make a decent brownie swoon.

Anyway, I heard her approaching and scrambled into an empty boot. Peering around the boot's upper rim, I watched her lift the edge of the bedspread. When she looked in with her great human eye, I was tempted to leap out and give her a good scare, but managed to resist.

"Huh," she muttered. "I could have sworn there was something down here."

She dropped the cloth. After a bit I heard her leave the room. At once I scrambled out and went back to work.

I had only been at it a few minutes when footsteps told me she was returning.

Back under the bed I went.

I could hear her moving around my refuge but didn't guess what she was up to—though if my nose hadn't been clogged by all that wretched dust, I might have figured it out from the smell. After a few minutes, she went back to her desk.

I waited until all was silent, then crept to the edge of the bed and lifted the spread to look out. She was hunched over her desk, working on a drawing.

I should have been more careful. I should have been more alert. But I was eager to return to my task. So I lowered the edge of the bedspread, then crawled through the clutter and debris to the far side.

As I scooted out, I felt a sticky mess grab my feet.

I was stuck in molasses! The wretched girl had spread a line of the gooey brown stuff all the way around her bed.

What made this strange is that it was the very same trick my sweet Sarah had played on me so many years ago.

At least the girl comes by her sneakiness honestly.

I shrieked with rage.

"Aha!" cried Alex. I heard her chair fall as she jumped out of it and came leaping over to the bed. Next thing I knew, her head was hanging over the edge of the bed and I was looking at her upside-down face.

"What in the world?" she cried. She scrambled across the bed to my side, reached down, and picked me up.

SHE PICKED ME UP! Grabbed me right around the middle and snatched me from the floor.

"Let me down, ya great lumbering slob of a girl!" I bellowed, pounding my fists against her fingers.

She tossed me to the bed and shook her hand as if she had been holding a rat.

Waving my fists and leaping up and down, I cried, "What did you do that for, ya disorderly, messy, negligent, slapdash, untidy, unfastidious, unsanitary creator of disorder?"

Alex blinked at me. But instead of answering my question, she said, "Are you some kind of elf?"

"Elf?" I cried, still leaping up and down. "*ELF?* Do I look all tall and willowy? I'm a brownie, as any fool can plainly see. A brownie who has been forced against his will to journey—at great trouble, I might add—to this disgusting midden of a room to bring some wee bit of tidiness to your disordered and chaotic life! And what have you done? What have you done? You've trapped me wi' molasses! Wretched girl. What's the matter wi' you?"

And after this cry from my heart, she had the nerve to reply, "What's the matter with *you*? Sneaking into a person's room and cleaning it up when you're not invited is creepy."

"I was *too* invited," I said.

"What a liar you are!" cried she.

"What a Messy Carruthers you are," I replied. "And you don't know everything, miss. I was sent here by one of your blood, which counts as an invitation if she is close enough . . . which she is."

"What are you talking about?"

"I was passed to you by your great-great-great-aunt Sarah McGonagall. She, being upon her deathbed, sent the family brownie—that being me—to her youngest female relative of age to receive me, that being you."

"Well, you're clearly in the wrong place. I'm a Carhart, not a McGonagall. And you can't be the family brownie because brownies don't exist."

"Rude! Rude, rude, rude, rude, rude! Sarah warned me about this. 'She's a modern girl,' she said, 'and may have a touch of the rudeness.' And she was right. And if you don't think I exist, then why are you talking to me? It must mean that you're crazy, eh?"

She blinked and took a step back. "Oh my god! Maybe I really am going crazy. What if Destiny is rubbing off on me? She has an imaginary friend. Can that be catching? No, that doesn't make any sense. But you can't be real. You can't be!"

"I'm real as toast, you great lolloping nonsense of a human!"

She shook her head. "I am going to leave the room. When I come back, you'll probably be gone. That will be good. But maybe I need to see a shrink. I don't like that idea, but I don't like the idea of being crazy, either. I'm going now. When I get back, please be gone."

And out of the room she goes.

The moment she left, I scurried back to the closet and climbed up to my hiding place. I try to respect the wishes of my human when I can. Even so, sooner or later she is going to have to accept that I am real.

FROM THE JOURNAL OF
ALEX CARHART

10/9 (Fri.)

OMG! There is something so weird going on at my house that I am afraid to write about it even here. If someone found it, they would think I was going crazy.

Actually, I'm afraid that maybe I really am going crazy. I wouldn't be the first in my family, according to my father. He still likes to tease Mom about her great-uncle Albert, who used to think he was an eggplant and was always worried about people trying to cook him.

~~I wonder if he saw little people, too?~~

Friday, October 9

When Alex came into her room after school today and found it once again tidy and spotless, she let out a little shriek.

Then, standing in the middle of the room, she said loudly, "All right, I admit you're real. Are you satisfied now?"

I climbed out of my shoe box and down the Wall of Mess to the floor. Then I scurried from closet door to bed so fast it appeared as if I just popped up in front of her.

"Aye, I'm satisfied, and glad of heart to be acknowledged as real. 'Tis most unpleasant to be a living, breathing creature and be thought unreal. I've not come to harm you, miss, nor to make you angry. I came because I had to, and because I yearn to be of service."

"I don't understand the 'I had to' part. I've already told you, I'm not a McGonagall. I'm a Carhart."

"Aye. And what was your father's mother's name before she married?"

"Chase," the young snip said smugly. "And don't say anything bad about my grandmother. She is a wonderful person."

"I'm sure she is. But tell me . . . what was *her* mother's maiden name?"

I could see Alex waver. "I don't have any idea," she said at last, sounding a bit irritable.

"Ha!" I cried, getting irritable myself. "No sense of family, have you? Rude, and irreverent as well. Well, I'll tell you what you should have known all along. Your great-grandmother on your father's side was a McGonagall—Agnes Ailsa Paisley McGonagall, to be precise."

"So why did this relative of mine assign you to me?" demanded Miss Mess, stamping her foot.

As I am writing this down, I begin to see some of the problem. It's not just that this Alex of mine is a messy young creature.

It's that she has the same temper I do.

Fortunately, I was spared having to answer when her lout of a brother bellowed, "Hey, Al! Hurry up and grab your sneakers. We have to leave for soccer NOW!"

"We'll talk about this later!" she said as she grabbed her trainers and raced out of the room.

I gathered from this that the Americans call trainers "sneakers." What an odd term. But what in the world is this "soccer" she was running off to?

Well, leave that to solve later. Right now I am going to go out and look for some mischief to do.

I would like to pull a prank on Miss Alex, but I do not think it would go well. She is too angry about my being here to find it funny if I were to stuff all her socks into her pillowcase.

Text messages between Ellen Carhart and Dennis Carhart

Ellen

Den, the weirdest thing happened this morning. When I was emptying the dishwasher and went to put away the silverware, I found the entire drawer rearranged.

Dennis

What do you mean?

Ellen

The forks and spoons had been moved around.

Dennis

What's so weird about that?

Ellen

We've put the utensils in the same place for twenty years! The kids swear they didn't move anything. It's almost enough to make me believe Alex's story about someone secretly cleaning up her room.

Dennis

Have you been sniffing the dishwasher soap, dear?

Ellen

Careful, buster, or you'll end up doing the dishes by hand, then sleeping in the doghouse. And remember, we don't have a dog!

Saturday, October 10

Alex was away for soccer practice for much of the day. (I have learned that this is the American term for what any sensible person would call "football.") When she came home, I gave her time to get cleaned up. (Thank goodness she is at least attentive to her own hygiene!) Then I went out to talk to her. As we were chatting, she said, "I've been trying to figure out who you sound like, and I've finally got it."

"And who might that be?" I asked.

"My mother works at an old folk's home, and there is an old lady there, a really old lady—"

"Are you sayin' I sound like an old lady?" I cried angrily.

"No! And the only reason you think that is because you interrupted before I could finish. So don't talk about *me* being rude."

I had naught I could say to that, for she was right. So I folded my hands primly in front of me and let her go on.

When she saw that I was resolved to listen, she said, "This old lady has an accent just like yours. I've been to the home with Mom a few times, so I've heard her."

Oh, my heart twinged with longing to once more hear the language as it ought to be spoken! I wonder if I can ever get Alex to take me to meet the old lady.

One awful incident per day should be sufficient. However, this day brought two, the first terrifying, the second horrifying. While a person might think those words mean the same thing, the two experiences were quite different. In the first, I was in fear of life and limb. In the second, though I was in no immediate danger, a surge of cold dread enveloped my heart.

Here is what happened.

After the Carharts departed for church, I decided to go outside for a bit of fresh air, as I had not been out since I first arrived. That did involve, of course, making sure that it was safe to pass through the kitchen. Fortunately, the dreaded cat was nowhere in sight. Out of caution, I pushed open Satan's Flap just a wee bit so I could make sure the demon spawn cat was not lurking just outside the door.

All clear, out I scooted.

'Twas a glorious day, and I felt free to romp and frolic a bit in the grass, which clearly had not been mowed for a while. After a bit of that I decided to lie in the shade beneath a tree to take a nap. Feeling at once that I was too exposed, I decided to cover myself with some fallen leaves. Made quite a nice bed, they did, and I fell into a deep and lovely sleep.

I have not had sufficient rest since I left Scotland.

I don't know how much time passed before I was woken by loud laughter. I nearly sprang to my feet, which would have revealed my hiding place, but caught myself in time. Pulling aside a leaf, I peeked out and saw that Alex and Bennett were playing soccer in the backyard. Well, not really playing soccer . . . more like just kicking the ball around. It gave me pleasure to see that both were quite adept at it and, as they were intent on what they were doing, I felt safe to sit up and watch more intently.

I was quite enjoying myself until Alex made a kick that went wild and sent the ball, which is nearly as tall as I am, hurtling directly at me! I leaped to my feet and sprinted away, but it was as if the cursed thing had my name on it. No matter how I zigged or zagged, it changed course with each bounce and kept coming at me. I knew if it landed on me it would knock me out, possibly kill me. It was hard on my heels, a great orb of death about to flatten me. So when I saw a hole ahead of me I plunged into it—much to the startlement of the rabbit who lived there.

"Have we met?" asked the poor bun, sounding confused.

"My apologies," I gasped. "I was fleeing an enemy!"

"The cat?" asked the rabbit, suddenly more sympathetic.

"No, a soccer ball!"

"Ah, yes," said my host, nodding solemnly. "I was nearly beaned by the thing myself just last week when I was out nibbling some grass. Feel free to stay here until the coast is clear."

As it turned out, the rabbit was quite a friendly fellow—which was just as well, as now that the Carharts were home, I didn't really dare return to the house until dark had fallen.

Which was when the second dreadful event occurred. Once I made it back into the room, I found Alex sitting at her desk. She had undone her braid and was brushing out her hair, and I must say that its richness and astonishing red color would have been worthy of the Enchanted Realm.

"I was wondering where you had been," she said when I slipped through the door.

Before I could answer, a voice that I recognized as belonging to her big brother said, "Hey, Al, can I talk to you for a minute?"

Without waiting for an answer, he pushed the door open. It was all I could do to scurry under the bed before he spotted me.

"Bennett!" Alex cried. "What are you doing here?"

His answer sent a chill down my spine.

"I was working on some poems, and I'm stuck. I was hoping you could help me."

"Why are you writing poetry?"

"I . . . I don't know for sure. It's just something that's come over me the last couple of days."

I peered out from beneath the bed and my heart twisted within me. I could see it in the lad's face, hear it in his voice. And when he read his poems aloud, I cringed.

I had hoped it could not cross the ocean.

I had hoped it had faded away.

My hopes were in vain.

I have brought the Curse of the McGonagalls with me to this house!

Maybe I should have let that soccer ball run over me after all.

THREE POEMS BY BENNETT CARHART

TO MARIE

Sweet Marie, my turtledove
You're my chocolate queen of love
All right
You're white
That's not the point
I want to be your boo tonight!

MY ACHING SOUL

Today at lunch I felt such pain,
I thought I'd never smile or laugh
    or be happy again.
At first it seemed like indigestion,
Then I asked myself a question.
Is this just the result of a bad burrito?
Or have I been bitten by love's mosquito?
Oh no! I've caught the itch of love,
My ookie wookie turtledove.

MY HEART BENEATH YOUR FOOT

My heart is squashed beneath your foot
Like a too-ripe tomato stepped on by a cow
And all that tomato juice, splattered
    and oozing out
Is like my blood. Oh! What shall I do now?

Monday, October 12

I have been in a lather all day, trying to think what to do about the curse.

There is no answer, of course. But I've never been in a house where it struck before, and I am appalled to think of what is to come.

To show how distressed I was, I was not even able to clean!

I did, however, get into the cellar. It is massive! And it is also like no cellar I have ever seen. I am used to cobwebs and dirt floors, a place cool, dark, and earthy. This cellar is vast (and dry!). It has furniture and games and another huge television set.

It's as if the Carharts actually like spending time down here!

The reason I was able to get in was that Mr. Carhart did not go to work today. Instead he went into the cellar, leaving the door open a crack.

I had to be careful, of course, but when I went down, I saw no sign of him. There was not much to map, as it is mostly open, but one room was quite mysterious to me. I suspect it is where he must have spent the day.

The sign on the door said MAN CAVE.

What in the world is that supposed to mean?

Cellar Area

Man Cave
(What goes on in here??)

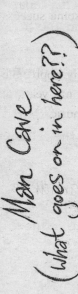

Is there really a cave on the other side of the door? That does not seem likely. But what is it? Was that where Mr. Carhart spent the day? Is he keeping someone prisoner in there? That does not seem likely, either. But what does it mean? I am mystified.

Tools & Workshop

Recreation / Play Area

Clearly a place of fun and frolic. Toys, games, comfy chairs. A mess, of course.

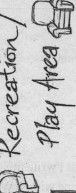

Stairs

Laundry Area
(Also, Junk Storage)

Big machines here. Big sinks, too. Makes me glad that doing laundry is not one of a brownie's tasks. I would probably drown.

Junk, junk, junk!

WILSON, WILSON, WILSON AND WILSON

2468 Providence Street · New Glasgow, CT

To: Anthony Wilson Jr., Vice President
From: Dennis Carhart, CPA
Date: October 12

Dear Tony,

It is not without some sorrow that I write this letter to confirm my resignation. I have enjoyed my time with WWW&W, and been made to feel most welcome here. However, as we discussed in your office today, my heart tells me the time has come to follow my passion.

I have been writing songs for years and had some success with them.

Now I need to do more.

Though I am sorry to leave the firm, and truly appreciate the many kindnesses you have shown me during my years at WWW&W, I must now follow the siren call of my music.

I have a song to sing-o!

Sincerely,

Dennis Carhart

(Former) CPA

Tuesday, October 13

When I came out to talk today, Alex was very upset. I asked her what was wrong, and her answer struck new horror into my heart.

"Dad quit his job. He's decided to chase his dream of being a songwriter. I'm afraid we're going to starve to death."

It's the curse, and no doubt about it! I now have great fears that the Carharts will lose their home and be put out upon the street. I try to tell myself that I have read too much of Charles Dickens (the greatest guide to human behavior that ever there was!) and this could not be in this time, in this great America.

I tell myself this, but I do not convince myself of it.

I feel such guilt. But what can I do? I am doomed to carry the curse with me, and I am doomed to stay in this house, where I will bring grief to the people I want only to serve.

Why, oh why, could I not have been sent to a house that had only women? Then all this would have been avoided.

It has been a long time since I have read the curse. In all my years with Sarah, I never had to worry about it. I will take it out tonight and examine it, to see if there is any ray of hope.

The Curse Bearer

Now do I, Greer M'Greer, Queen of Scotland's Enchanted Realm, also known as the Queen of Shadows, lay this curse upon you, Seamus Cairns, and upon all your descendants as well.

First, you shall be brownie-bound to the family of Ewan McGonagall until such time as the curse upon that family shall end.

Second, your binding shall be in this fashion: You shall go to the youngest female who is of age, that being ten years or more. Attached to her shall you be until the moment of her death, at which time you must make your way to your next mistress, who shall be the youngest female of the McGonagall line who is of age, be she pauper or princess, fair or foul, tidy or a slattern. And you serve and protect until the time of her death, when once again you shall go to the youngest female of the line who is old enough to have you.

And so it shall be forevermore, for you and for the eldest male of each generation that follows, the chain unbroken until what was lost to me shall be restored. But oh, what a burden on the houses you inhabit shall come with your service! For each of you shall carry the Curse of the McGonagalls, and when you arrive every male in the house shall be afflicted with it.

May their tears be enough to water a thousand fields and their sighs be enough to fill the sails of a thousand ships.

So say I, Greer M'Greer. And so shall it be!

Tuesday, October 13 (late at night)

I read the curse three times but found no hope. The
only way to lift it is to return to the queen what was lost.
But I canna imagine any way in which that can be done.
I DESPAIR!

FROM THE JOURNAL OF
ALEX CARHART

10/14 (Wed.)

I seriously hope no one ever reads this because if they do, they'll decide I'm totally crazy.

Hmmm. I suppose it's possible that I am. I mean, if you think about it hard enough, you can imagine that everything you know is just some delusion and you're really just a brain in a tank somewhere.

But that's too scary to think about for long.

Besides, I don't think it's true.

So if I am not crazy (and I don't think I am), then the brownie is real!

SERIOUSLY!

Now that I've had a chance to think about it, I've decided this is the coolest thing that ever happened to me.

I mean, I have a magical creature living in my closet! Sure, the little dude can be annoying. Even so, having him here is the neatest thing in the history of my life!

So that's the good thing.

The bad thing is that last night Mom and Dad had a big fight about Dad quitting his job. Mom is freaking out and I can't blame her. He didn't even talk to her before he did this!

Also, Bennett is starting to act really weird. Last night at dinner he said he was thinking about quitting soccer!

When Mom asked why, he said, "I need more time for my poetry."

If Mom had actually read any of his poetry, she probably would have spit out her herbal tea when he said that.

I figured Dad would be mad, since he's very big on sports. But he just clapped his hand on Ben's shoulder and said, "I understand, son. I understand."

And I guess he does, given that he just quit his job for his songwriting.

Now that I think about it, maybe having a brownie move into my closet was the least weird thing that's happened this week!

Wednesday, October 14

I have been in the midst of a major fret all day, wondering whether to say ought to Alex of the curse.

Given how upset she is already, it can only make matters worse.

I would leave if I could, but that is not to be. I knew the bringing of the curse was possible, but never having been in a house where it actually happened, I had no idea how bad it would be.

What makes it worse is that things are getting better between the girl and me. When she returned from school this afternoon, she said, "Come on out, brownie. I need to know more about why you're here."

Thanking her for the invitation, I climbed out of my shoe box.

"Do you want me to lift you down?" she asked.

"Nae, miss, I prefer not to be picked up. I'll make my own way."

As I scrambled to the floor, she said, "You're very athletic."

"We brownies need to be strong to do our work. If I were human height, I would be able to lift your father's car!"

This was a bit of a brag, but as it was true, I didna think it was too bad to say it.

When I reached the floor, she said, "Would you rather sit on my desk or on my bed?"

I looked at her desk and shuddered.

"Right. Silly question. Sorry."

She picked up the chair from her desk and set it beside the bed. I climbed the bedspread and sat down tailor style. When I was settled, she said, "So tell me why this distant relative of mine assigned you to me?"

I was not yet ready to explain the curse. So I chose to use a different word. "It wasn't assigned so much as obeying the terms of my family's ancient, er . . . agreement with your family. It states that when my human passes on, I must go to the youngest female of the line—"

"The youngest would be my little sister, Destiny!"

"I'll thank you not to interrupt! As I was trying to say, I must go to the youngest female of the line who is *old enough to take me on*! As Destiny is too young, that happens to be you. It's not like I wanted to come to this barbarian wilderness. It's just that, things being what they are, I didn't have any choice. So here I am, much to your good fortune, and bound to you for as long as we both shall live. Of course, as it is likely I will outlive you, I am—"

"That's not very nice. When are you expecting me to die?"

"Oh, not for many and many a year. It's just that humans don't last as long as brownies do."

She scowled at me. After a moment, she said, "You keep talking about an agreement. I didn't agree to anything."

"Of course you didn't! This agreement was made nearly three centuries ago."

"Are you claiming you're three hundred years old?"

"No, though I do have a bit over a century and a half to my name. The binding was first laid on my father, Seamus Cairns, and passed on to me at the time of his death. I am now tied to your family, and to you specifically, until either one of us shall die. Just imagine how lovely it will be to have your things all neat and tidy every day!"

"But I like them the way they are!"

"Well, it makes no difference. I'm here now, and it's here I must stay."

"So you're saying I don't have any choice in this?"

"Of course you don't have a choice. It's a family matter. No one gets a choice when it comes to things like that. We're no more free of the past than we are of breathing."

"But I don't like you messing with my stuff."

This peeved me greatly. "I am not messing. I am unmessing."

She rolled her eyes. "You are going to drive me nuts!"

"And you are already driving me quite mad," I snapped

back. "But there's naught we can do about it. Though I am personally quite tidy, I cannot deny that fate takes some messy turns. However, the fact that life can be quite messy doesn't mean your bedroom has to be!"

Feeling my temper getting the better of me, I leaped off the bed and stomped over to the closet.

Sadly, stomping is not very effective when you are scarcely a foot high.

back. "But there's naught we can do about it. Though I am personally quite tidy, I cannot deny that fate turns some misadventures. However, the fact that . . . doesn't mean your bedroom has to be."

Today when Alex arrived home from school, I went out to join her, as has become our habit. When I was seated in my usual spot, she said, "I've got some questions for you."

Folding my hands, I said, "I will answer if I can."

"For starters, what's your name? I can't keep calling you 'brownie.'"

I'm not ashamed to say I felt a lump in my throat as I said, "My name is Angus Cairns."

"Do you want me to call you Angus or Mr. Cairns?"

"Angus is fine, miss."

She made a face. "I don't like 'miss.' Call me Alex, please."

"All right . . . Alex."

"Next question: Do you really have nowhere else to go?"

I shook my head and made my saddest face. I have learned that this is quite effective on humans. It has to do with my big brown eyes, especially when I let tears brim at the bottom of them.

"Well, if you're going to stay here, we need some rules so we can get along without killing each other. I have been studying brownies and—"

"How did you do that?"

"I Googled it, of course."

"You did what?"

"You know, Googled it. Did an Internet search."

I felt like she was talking a different language.

Alex must have seen my confusion, because she said, "You do know what the Internet is, right?"

When I shook my head, she seemed as surprised as I was confused. She sighed, then said, "Let me see if I can explain."

When she was done, all I could say was, "It sounds like magic to me. Are you sure there's no witchcraft involved?"

"Nope, just science."

I realized for the first time how fast the world had been changing while I lived in Sarah's cottage up in the highlands.

"Anyway," she said, "all I had to do was type in 'Brownie,' and once I got past the kind you eat—"

"The kind you eat?!"

"Yeah, you know, brownies."

"You humans are eating us now?" I cried in horror.

"Don't be silly. A brownie is a kind of . . . oh, I don't know. Sort of like a thick, squashed-down piece of choco-late cake. They're delicious."

"Why are they called brownies?"

"Duh. Because they're brown! Also, there's the Girl Scout kind of Brownies, which you obviously are not. But

I found lots of information about your kind of brownie, though most of the pictures didn't look anything like you."

"We like to stay mysterious," I said.

She smiled. "I think it's cool that I get to know a real brownie. Anyway, I understand now about you wanting to keep the room clean. But if we're going to get along, we need to have a few rules. First off, my desk space is mine and I want you to leave it as it is. Agreed?"

I glanced at the desk and shuddered, but nodded.

"Also, you'll stay out of my private things, right?"

"Just to be clear, what would those be?"

"For now, my journal and my top drawer. Also, you have to promise not to watch when I change my clothes. I don't want to spend the rest of my life having to go into the bathroom to change!"

"That's fine with me. I've no interest in seeing your people parts. But how am I to know when you're about to change?"

She thought, then said, "When I'm going to change, I'll knock two times on the closet door. That means don't come out. When I knock again, that will mean it's all right."

"As long as you promise never to forget to knock when you're done, it's a deal."

I licked my thumb and held it out to her.

"What are you doing?"

"Lick your thumb and I'll give you a spit swear never to watch you change."

She made a face but licked her thumb.

"Now press your thumb to mine."

She did.

"There. Now you can be sure."

"Well, all right," she said. "Let's see how things go."

So we seem to have a truce of sorts. And that feels good.

But oh, I ache to have a place where I am not just tolerated but truly wanted and welcome, as I was with my dear Sarah.

I want to have a home.

WILSON, WILSON, WILSON AND WILSON
2468 Providence Street · New Glasgow, CT

To: Dennis Carhart
From: Tony Wilson
Re: Take some time to think!
Date: 10/15

Den—

I had a long talk with the old man last night. He was pretty steamed by the way you resigned on such short notice, especially after he had just given you a raise. He was also kind of hurt. (Really, Den, resigning is one thing, but doing it without giving us time to look for a replacement was really unprofessional, as I'm sure you know.)

The thing is, angry as Dad was, he also really hates to see you go. You've been here a long time, and we both really value your work. After I got him calmed down, we came up with this possibility: Why don't you take the next few weeks to rest and think things through. If at the end of that time you still feel the same way, then we will bid you farewell with no hard feelings—though I will have to ask you to come into the office to help train whoever we hire to take your place.

Speaking as your oldest friend, I know your finances are not all they might be. It's not easy raising three kids these days. If you decide to come back, I might even be able to talk the old man into giving you an additional raise. I hope you will.

Tony

When Alex came home this afternoon, I went out to talk, as is now our habit. I was sitting on the bed and we had exchanged a few pleasant words when Bennett moped into the room.

The big lout didn't even knock, so I had no time to do a scurry. Stuck, I did the only other thing I could and froze, pretending I was naught but some doll or toy.

The lad was dressed all in black. He had papers in his hand, so I was fair sure he was carrying more of his pathetic verses. I felt a twinge of guilt, since his condition is entirely due to my presence.

That pity didn't last long, given what happened next.

The wretched lad saw me, walked to the bed, and picked me up! Then he said, "Good grief, Al. Why do you have such an ugly doll?"

I wanted to bite his thumb and shout, "I'm nae a doll, you great lummox! I'm a brownie. A brownie, fierce and proud!"

But I could not, of course.

Then Alex made it worse by telling him, "Oh, it's like those troll dolls I used to collect . . . you know, so ugly that it's cute."

I was quivering inside by that point. Being called a doll is one thing. Being called a troll was just too much!

When he finally set me down—tossed me, actually—he inflicted his latest batch of horrid poetry on Alex, then left the room.

As soon as he was gone, I sprang to my feet and shouted in my quietest voice, "Troll! TROLL?! I am nae a troll! I'm a brownie through and through, as well you know, you wicked girl."

"And did you want me to tell Bennett that? I could have told him that you're a brownie and you were only acting all stiff so he wouldn't know you were real. Would that have been better?"

I wanted to pitch a fit at that, but I knew she was right. She had saved me from a big problem.

"But why did you have to say I was a troll? Trolls are great slobbering stony things from the north. They're a thousand times bigger than a brownie, with only a tenth of a brownie's brain. They'd as soon step on you as say hello. I am nothing like a troll!"

"I didn't say you were a troll. I said you were like a troll doll. Here, I'll show you."

She went to the big wooden chest that is crammed with her old toys and rummaged around in it a bit, throwing several things onto the floor behind her as she did.

Honestly, I don't know if there's any civilizing this girl.

Anyway, suddenly she turns around with this . . . this . . . naked plastic THING. It had bulging eyes, a wild spray of purple hair, a big foolish grin, a bulging belly, and a nose that looked like half a potato. I have drawn it to show how insulting this was!

Angus

"You think I look like *that*?" I shrieked.

"Don't be silly, Angus. You don't look like this at all. I'm just showing it to you as an example of something that's so ugly it's cute."

"So which am I? Ugly or cute?"

"Neither. You're mostly just annoying."

And that was all we said for the night.

FROM THE JOURNAL OF ALEX CARHART

10/16 (Fri.)

Angus got all upset tonight because I compared him to a troll doll. It was kind of annoying, but also kind of funny. Only I didn't let him know that, because he would only have gotten more upset.

What I'm really worried about is Dad. He is the one who usually keeps things fun, and he can always crack us up if things get too tense. But he has been moping around for the last few days, almost like Bennett.

If he starts dressing all in black, I'm really going to get nervous.

I asked Mom about him, but she didn't want to talk about it. "Your father is going through a phase" was all she would say, though later I heard her mutter, "Why couldn't he just have bought a red sports car?"

I know she's really upset and distracted since she hasn't even noticed how neat and clean my room is. That's all thanks to Angus, of course, but I still would have liked it if she had said something about it.

I wish I knew what the heck is going on around here.

No school today, of course, but Alex was still gone most of the time as she had soccer practice. When she came home, she said loudly, "How lovely my room looks! Except for my desk, of course, which is quite a mess. I do hope that's all right."

"Thank you, miss," I called. "'Tis nice to be appreciated."

Then I scrambled out for our daily chat, which I have come to look forward to.

Alas, it only took about two minutes for it to go sour. That was because after we exchanged a few pleasantries, she said, "I've been thinking about it, and it might be fun to have a pet brownie."

I leaped to my feet. Jumping up and down and shaking my fists, I shrieked, "Pet? PET?! Take the foul word back, ya horrid girl! I made a spit swear to make you happy. Now you turn around and spit in my face. I am a brownie, fierce and proud, and I AM NAE A PET!"

With that, I jumped down to the floor and scurried back to the closet.

"You have a pretty big temper for such a little man!" she shouted. Which did not make things any better.

Now that I've settled down, I am not sure which was

worse—what she said, or the way I pitched a fit after she said it.

I have to remember she is a barbarian and not used to civilized ways.

Also, I need to work on my temper.

HOW TO BE A BETTER BROWNIE

 by Buttercup MacKenzie

It is the curse of our kind that, though we are thoughtful, loving, and helpful by nature, we are also quick-tempered and slow to forgive. It is for this reason that I have prepared this pamphlet, which I hope will provide guidance for the brownie who discovers that his or her temper has placed him or her in a situation of isolation.

(If I may be allowed a personal note, I would add that the modern demand for me to write "his or her" is enough to make me want to fling my pot of ink against the wall! But I digress. . . .)

Anyway, should you, dear fellow brownie, find yourself on the verge of losing control, here are the steps I would recommend to you.

First, count to ten. This is an old and time-honored bit of advice. And it does contain a certain amount of wisdom, as it helps prevent an immediate eruption. However, I must report from personal experience that counting to ten is generally insufficient. I myself must get to at least 537 before the desire to leap upon someone and start gnawing holes in his or her face begins to subside.

Sunday, October 18

Alex is away this morning, as the family has gone to church.

I've thought about my explosion yesterday afternoon with much regret.

The best I can manage right now is to resolve to be a better brownie. Not in terms of cleaning and doing my work. I'm already doing twice what a brownie ought just to keep this place under control. But I begin to see that my temper is a curse of its own, and something I need to work on.

Also, I must keep in mind that the girl is ignorant of my ways. I cannot always blame her for her lack of under-standing. For instance, I never made it clear to her that I am not a pet . . . though it ought to be obvious to anyone who thinks about it for more than a second!

Well, now that she knows how I feel about it, if she ever dares call me a pet again, I'll be justified in pitching a fit that will make the lightbulbs burst in their sockets! But first-time trespasses should get a pass.

Hmmm, I rather like that! It could almost be an old saying.

Anyway, when Alex gets home today, I will come out to talk to her again, in the hope that we can do better.

In the meantime, there is cleaning to do. (Of course!)

Also, in the fuss of traveling and getting settled, I have been neglecting my mischief. I need to set that right. That's part of being a better brownie, too! I think I can get some in while the Carharts are off at church.

LATER

Mischief plans severely hampered by presence of CAT. Must figure out what to do about this.

But that's not the most important thing to talk about right now. The bigger thing is that after Alex returned, I waited for her to get settled, then came out to join her.

She was at her desk, working on a drawing, and didn't notice me at first. So once I was on the bed, I said softly, "Ahem."

She turned and gave me a sour look. "Oh. It's you."

As if it could be anyone else!

Folding my hands and looking the proper brownie, I said, "I'm sorry I lost my temper yesterday. My short fuse is a curse, and not the only one I bear. I have made a vow to work on it. But you must understand, too, that it was a horrid thing you said to me. I'm nae a cat, nor a fluffy bunny, nor a wee bird to be put in a cage. I may not be human, but I'm a person naetheless, and not to be a pet."

She sighed. "I know. I've been feeling bad about what I said yesterday, and I'm sorry. But you didn't have to get so angry. You could have just told me it was wrong."

As I had already apologized, I thought it was rude of her to say this. I near pitched another fit. But I remembered the wise words of Buttercup MacKenzie and closed my eyes and began to count.

After a moment, she said, "What are you doing?"

"Counting."

"Why are you counting?"

"I'm trying not to lose my temper!"

"Oh, like counting to ten. My mother has told me I should do that, too."

"Will ya be quiet? I'm still trying to keep the fit from bustin' out of me!"

She fell silent, and after a while I was able to take a deep breath.

"All right," I said, opening my eyes. "I can talk again. Sorry about that wee outburst."

She had her back to me, and when she turned to face me, I saw tears on her cheeks.

It made me feel like the worst brownie in the world.

"I was just trying to be nice," she said.

"And I was just trying not to pitch a fit," I said. "It's not easy, but I'm working on it. I have a fierce bad temper."

"How high did you count?"

"One thousand, two hundred and forty-six."

And that was where we left things for the night.

FROM THE JOURNAL OF
ALEX CARHART

10/18 (Sun.)

    I'm not speaking to Angus right now. He really needs to work on his temper.

    In other news: Things are worse with Dad. He spends most of his time down in the studio now. And the problem isn't just between him and Mom. Yesterday he had a big fight with Pete!

    This is serious. Dad and Pete have been writing songs together for years, and I've never heard them fight before. As near as I could make out, it was because Dad wants to start writing the words to his songs himself. But that's always been Pete's job, so he was mad. I don't blame him . . . especially given some of the things Dad has written. They're awful!

    Bennett is getting weirder, too. The only time we've seen him for the last couple of days is when he comes slinking out of his room for supper. He's dressing all in black and is incredibly mopey.

    What the heck is going on around here?!

Monday, October 19

This afternoon, after I apologized to Alex for my wee tantrum, she said, "Angus, what have you been eating?"

"How kind of you to ask," I replied a bit tartly. "It's a good thing I am nae a pet, which we have now established. If I were, I would long since have been stinking up your closet with my moldering corpse, gone from this world for lack of anyone bothering to feed me."

She scowled. "Well, you're clearly not fading away. So you do eat, right?"

"I do indeed."

"Well, what? And where have you been getting it?"

This was a bit uncomfortable, as I was not sure how she would take the answer.

"Well?" she said again after a minute.

"I have been snitching things from the kitchen, as is my right for the work that I do! But my diet is rather limited. I can't open your refrigerator, so the best I can manage is things in boxes and bags . . . cereal and chips mostly. No one can begrudge me that, for I eat but a small amount. But it's too much salt and sugar, which is nae good for my heart. Oh, how I long for a bit o' the blessed haggis."

"What in the world is haggis?"

"Oh, 'tis a lovely savory pudding. You start with the stomach of a sheep, then stuff it with a mixture of the sheep's heart, liver, and lungs (all chopped up, of course), along with some oatmeal, suet, spices—"

"Stop!" she shrieked.

Then she began to make very loud and disgusting fake vomiting sounds.

I had not realized Americans have such sensitive stomachs.

When she finally calmed down, she said, "I promise I'll bring you food from now on, Angus. I'm sorry I didna ask you sooner."

It was my turn to scowl. "Are you making fun o' me?"

"No! Why?"

"You said 'didna' rather than 'didn't.' I thought you were makin' fun o' my accent."

She blushed a bit. "Mom says I'm a natural mimic. I tend to pick up on the way people around me are speaking. When we go on vacation to Canada, I come back speaking like a Canadian. And if I visit Mom at work and talk to the woman there who sounds like you, I come back sounding a little like her." She made a face. "Bennett-the-Booger says I pick up accents so easily because I have a weak personality."

"He's a booger, all right," I agreed.

Anyway, the upshot of all this is that she will bring me food from now on. Which will make things a bit easier.

She remains a slob (this is a word I recently learned from listening to Bennett-the-Booger), but I am starting to see that she is a kindhearted one, and that counts for something.

SONG LYRIC BY DENNIS CARHART

Oh, bury me not on the lone prairie
Cuz I ain't dead, as you can see.
My heart still beats, and my stomach burns
With lots of acid, which means it churns.

Oh, I loved deep, and I loved true.
I loved so hard, my face turned blue.
But that sweet love was spurned, so now I weep
Cuz my true love said I was a creep.

I flung myself over a cliff
Because we had a lovers' tiff.
And when I landed on the rocks below
I knew my love would have to go!

From a set of seventeen song recordings submitted to
Thracks Trax Music

Tuesday, October 20

I write this after a long and exhausting day.

It started when I went out to begin my work this morning and saw that Alex had left her research report on her desk. She had worked hard on that report, and I knew she would be in big trouble with her teacher if she was late in handing it in, as she has already missed many assignments. I knew *this* because I have overheard her mother speak to her about it almost every day, usually quite loudly.

I think Mrs. Carhart might do well to read *How to Be a Better Brownie*.

It's too bad the print would be too tiny for her eyes.

(Despite the above, I have much sympathy for Mrs. Carhart. Having a child like Alex must be a great trial.)

Though this situation definitely qualified as a mess for Alex, strictly speaking it is not part of my duties to help with a problem like this. Should I try to take it to her? It might make her feel better about me being here.

After much fussing and cudgeling of my brains (I mean that quite literally—I pounded upon my head trying to talk myself out of it), I rolled the essay into a neat curl and tied it with a bit of string. The house was quiet— the young Carharts at school, Mrs. Carhart at work, Mr. Carhart locked away in his Man Cave, which turned out to be his "studio," where he pens his wretched songs. So the only one I needed to worry about was Bubbles (Sweet Lords of the Hunt, what a name for the monster!), and I was hoping the beast was outside.

No such luck as that. When I got to the kitchen, who did I see with his face in his food bowl? Bubbles, of course. But I was a brownie with a job to do, and not about to take any nonsense from a mere cat. So I set aside the rolled-up report and braced myself. This was not Angus-just-arrived-and-all-worn-out. This was Angus-on-a-mission.

It was time to settle this for good.

The cat looked up, saw me, and crouched.

I crouched, too.

The cat sprang.

I sprang at the same instant, my mighty leap taking me far higher than his. The cat landed beneath me, and I landed on his back.

Unfortunately, I had landed backwards! I lunged up, grabbed Bubbles's tail, and used it to swing into the air.

This time I came down right way forward. As I did, the beast yowled and reared like the horses in the old Westerns I used to watch with Sarah.

I sank my hands into his fur, dug my heels into his sides, then cried, "All right, Bubbles, it's time to decide who's in charge here!"

The cat bucked, yowled, twisted, and squirmed.

I held on as if clutching the secret of life. (In a way, I was, since I knew that if I fell off his back, his claws would soon be doing unspeakable things to my innards.)

The cat galloped forward, yowling as if his tail was on fire.

I couldn't help myself. As we tore through the dining room and the living room, I swatted at his backside and shouted, "Yahooooo! Ride 'em, Brownie!"

Angus

Suddenly the cat skidded to a halt. He flung himself sideways, then onto his back.

I kept my grip, holding on like Janet clutching Tam Lin in the old tale. Though I was tiring, I dared not let go. My only hope was to hold on until Bubbles was exhausted.

The creature finally stopped, gasping for breath. That was when I played my last card. Pulling myself forward, I whispered in his ear, "Ya didn't expect to meet your match today, did ya, ya daft fur ball?"

The cat froze. I suspect no one had ever before talked to him in his own language.

"That's right," I said. "I know the language of the beasts. That first night you had the best of me, but now I've the better of you. And what I need to tell you is this: Miss Alex is in a mess. This morning she left behind some papers that are important for her to have in school. I am ready to bring them to her, but I need help. Are you willing to help me? For the sake of your girl, will you get me to that school?"

The cat held still for a long moment, then replied, "Yes."

"Well, then let's be out the door and on our way. The sooner we deliver these papers, the better. Though first we have to stop so I can pick it up, of course."

"Of course," said the cat.

"I'm going to get down. You'd best not try anything

when I do. Remember, we are now a team if we're to help Alex."

Bubbles made an irritated sound but said nothing more.

I slid down, ready to leap away if necessary.

Normally I don't like to deal with cats. They're finicky and can't always be trusted. But as my dear Sarah used to tell me, "Angus, you can't choose where the ball lands. You have to play it where it lies." (She was very proud that golf was invented in Scotland.)

Happily, I didn't have any more trouble with Bubbles. In fact, he was quite helpful. After I retrieved Alex's work and was about to mount him again, he said, "You should wait until we're outside. Otherwise the flap is apt to knock you onto your butt."

I thanked him for this bit of wisdom.

As it turned out, it was a good thing I had taken the time to tame the cat, since he knew a backyard route to school, which was definitely the best way for us to get there without my being seen.

When I thanked Bubbles for this, he said, "Do you think you're the only one who doesn't want to be seen? I've no desire to be spotted with a little man riding on my back!"

I nearly pitched a fit but started to count instead.

After we passed through a small wooded lot that led

to the edge of the playground, Bubbles stopped and said, "This is where you get off. I am not going to cross that wide open space carrying you as if I were some tiny horse!"

"That's fine, and I thank you for bringing me this far."

Despite his objection to being seen with me, the cat seemed to have taken the team idea to heart, for he said, "Do you want me to wait for you?"

"Thank you, but no," I replied. "I'll get a ride home with Alex. Or walk if I must. There'll be no hurry, and now that I know your route, I can do it without being noticed."

"Then I'll be off. Good luck!"

The playground was indeed a wide space to cross, with almost nowhere to hide. At least there were no classes outside. Taking a deep breath, I went into full scurry mode. Usually I only use my scurrying power to cross a room, nae such a great distance as this. The trip took a huge burst of energy, and I was fair winded when I reached the far side.

As I leaned against the building, trying to catch my breath, I realized I hadn't thought this through. How was I to get inside the place?

Well, the first thing to do was find Alex's room. That was simple enough. I just made my way along the foundation, pressing myself tight to the concrete, until I could sense Alex nearby.

As the building was built of brick, I knew I could climb it. But I was going to need both hands. I undid the string with which I had tied up the paper and used it to bind the roll to my back. The paper was getting a bit squashed, but there was no help for that.

Now that my hands were free, I leaped to the bricks and started to climb.

Glory be to goodness, the windows were open! They were an odd kind of window, low and wide. They didn't slide up, as I was used to, but tilted out. Happily, the opening was big enough for me to slip through. However, I couldn't go in with the class there, as someone was almost certain to see me. So I clung to the wall, peering into the room with my eyes just above the ledge.

I quickly spotted Alex.

I had been hanging there for several minutes when the teacher clapped her hands and said, "Time for lunch! Everyone line up."

As soon as they were out the door, I scrambled through the window, then scooted to my girl's desk. I shinnied up a leg, climbed on top, then took the roll of papers from my back and flattened it out.

It rolled right back up, which I should have expected.

I unrolled it again, then stood on one end.

The other end rolled up, knocking against my knees.

Cursing a bit, I leaned over the edge of the desk. It had a top, bottom, and three sides but was open where the student sits. I assume this is so things can easily be put in and taken out. Only it would be a task to put anything new in Alex's desk . . . it was already crammed to bursting.

Sweet Lords of the Hunt, the messes this child makes!

I dug around and found a big eraser, a quarter, a smooth stone the size of my head, and a plastic turtle. I hauled them up to the desktop, then used them to hold down the corners of Alex's assignment.

I had just finished, and was planning to scoot over to the window and make my exit, when I heard the teacher come back in!

I did the only thing I could and went over the edge of the desk and into the mess inside. It was no easy thing to squeeze into that miniature junkyard! When I had gone as far as I thought I could, my head was still sticking out. So I burrowed deeper, wedging myself between a book and something soft and squishy that I didn't want to think about. I stopped when the point of a pencil hit my bum.

And there I stayed. It's possible I have been in a more uncomfortable position sometime in my life, but if so, I can't remember it.

I had hoped the teacher would leave to pick up her class and I could escape then. No such luck. Some other teacher delivered them to the door!

As Alex's chair scraped back, I heard her mutter, "What the . . . ?" She bent and peered into the desk, then hissed, "Angus! What are you doing here?"

I shook my head and pressed my finger to my lips. She

nodded—thank goodness the girl is quick—and took her seat. After a while she moved around, and I heard her clear her throat. I saw that she had positioned her backpack so I could climb into it.

I shuddered, remembering the mess I had seen tumble out of it before. But it couldn't be worse than remaining where I was. I scooted backwards and slid into the pack, which is where I stayed until she carried me home at the end of the school day.

Back in her room, she laid her pack on the bed and opened the end. "Thanks for bringing that report," she said as I crawled out. "You saved my butt!"

"You're quite welcome," I replied, pulling something disgusting off of my tunic. "But if you don't mind, I'll go back to the closet now. I've had about all I can take for one day."

I dragged myself up to my shoe box, where I quickly fell into a deep sleep.

I'm not sure how long I napped. I awoke about an hour ago and have been writing this ever since.

FROM THE JOURNAL OF
ALEX CARHART

10/20 (Tues.)

Angus did the nicest thing today. He brought me the
research report that I had left at home!

It must have been scary to make the trip to my school all
on his own. He definitely got me out of huge trouble by doing it!

I have to think of something nice to do to thank him.

In other news, the hair has hit the chair! By which I mean
the end of my hair is finally all the way down my back. Can't sit
on it yet, but I'll get there soon.

This afternoon Alex said, "Angus, you need to stay in the closet for a little while. I'm going to have Bennett help me with something, and I know you don't want him to see you."

I was burning with curiosity, of course, but I did as she asked.

I heard her knock on Bennett's door but could only catch some of their words . . . enough to know that she was asking, and then demanding, that he go to the attic with her.

A few minutes after that, they came back into the room. Between them they were carrying a great pink concoction of a dollhouse.

Bennett was looking pretty cranky. But when Alex said, "Thanks, Ben. I bet you can get a poem out of this," he brightened up and said, "Great idea!"

Once he had left, I climbed down from the closet.

"What is that thing?" I asked.

"It's for you! I thought it would be a more comfortable place for you to stay than the closet."

"But it's pink!"

"Well, it's the right size, isn't it?"

"Yes, but it's pink. I can't live in a pink house. I'm a

brownie, nae a fairy! Besides, it doesn't have any front. You can look right in!"

"Well, you can look right out of the closet and see me!"

"As if I want to! And you know I'm not to be seen by the rest of your family."

"I'll hang a sheet over the front. That way you'll have your privacy."

"And how will you explain having the thing in your room to begin with?"

"I'll tell Mom it's for a secret art project. That will explain the sheet, too. Do you want it or not? I was just trying to be nice."

My new home

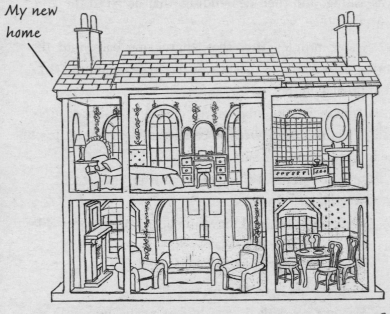

Angus

The girl has an answer for everything. But I have to admit that it warmed my heart to have her thinking of me this way.

Undignified as it is, I will try living in the Pink Horror. At the least it will give me more space than the shoe box. And perhaps by keeping it prim and proper, I can set a good example for the slovenly Miss Alex.

We did turn the open side to the wall, which makes things better.

Even so, I still made her hang a sheet over it.

October 21

Dear Coach Gorman,

I know I haven't been doing that well at practice lately, and I apologize. The truth is, I'm distracted by all the beautiful poetry that keeps swirling around in my head. I just don't think my heart is in soccer anymore, so I've decided to quit the team for the good of everyone.

Sincerely,
Bennett Carhart (Poet)

Yesterday I told Alex that the furniture that came with the Pink Horror was a problem.

"Why is that?" she asked.

"Well, it's hard, which is uncomfortable. It's plastic, which is disgusting. Worst of all, my bum doesn't fit in most of the chairs."

She laughed, which I thought was rude, then said, "Yes, Barbie's butt is definitely smaller than yours."

"Who is Barbie?" I asked, suddenly wondering if there was another wee person about the house after all.

"You never heard of Barbie? Where have you been living for the last hundred years?"

"In Scotland, as you well know."

"Well, I bet they have Barbies in Scotland."

"Aye, we have Barbies and Mollies and Marys and Fionas and all sorts of other female types. But we don't make special furniture for every girl that comes along!"

"No, silly—"

"I am nae silly!"

She rolled her eyes at me (a very unappealing habit). "No, *Angus*. Barbie is a fashion doll. I gave most of mine to Destiny a while ago, but if I can find one, I'll show it to you."

I didn't think finding anything likely, given how disorganized she is, so I forgot about it for the time being. But it was to prove a great embarrassment to me when I went to bed that night.

I had spent part of the evening having a conversation with Bubbles, who turns out to be not a bad sort for a cat.

We have a space in the guest bedroom where we meet to talk without being noticed. I did have to clear out an appalling amount of dust from under the bed to make it fit for a sit, but now it's quite pleasant.

We started by telling each other some jokes. Alas, that didn't go very well. As it turns out, brownies and cats have very different senses of humor. Cat jokes are mostly about how stupid mice are. Brownie jokes are mostly wit and wordplay. However, Bubbles did tell me some amusing stories about the Carharts, such as the time Bennett was locked out of the house in only his underwear. So we did have a few good laughs.

I have to say, a cat's laugh is an odd sound.

We also talked about some more personal matters, such as our tempers. It turns out that Bubbles is now on his third veterinarian due to bad behavior during routine appointments.

We are considering forming an anger-management group.

When I returned to Alex's room, it was dark and she had gone to bed. I was drowsy myself. Half asleep,

I dragged myself up the stairs of the Pink Horror to the bedroom where I had placed my shoe box, which is far more comfortable than that plastic bed.

When I climbed into the shoe box, I got the shock of my life!

"Alex!" I screamed. "Alex, there's a dead girl in my bed!"

Normally I am not one for screaming. However, I feel strongly that climbing into your own bed and finding yourself beside a cold, hard body is fair reason to let out a good shriek.

I heard Alex rouse.

"What's going on?" she asked, sounding groggy.

"There's a body in my bed!"

The wretched child laughed!

"What's so funny?" I demanded.

She switched on the lamp that sits on her nightstand. "That's not a body. It's a Barbie doll! I told you I was going to get one out so you could see what they look like."

Oh, didn't I felt a right fool. Even so, I think it was a fair mistake. But now that the light was on and I got a good look at the thing, I was horrified all over again.

"No human being looks like that!" I cried. "What are they puttin' into girls' heads, givin' them dolls like this?" I studied her more closely and added, "And why does she have a mustache?"

Alex made a face. "There's a reason I call my brother Bennett-the-Booger. He did that with a Sharpie."

"Well, why doesn't she have any clothes on? It's nae decent."

Alex sighed and took the awful naked plastic thing out of my shoe box.

"All right?" she asked.

"Yes. Thank you."

She returned to her bed, switched off the lamp, then called softly, "Good night, Angus."

"Good night," I growled.

As I lay down to sleep, I could hear her chuckling.

"It's nae funny!" I shouted. Only I knew that, really, it was. If she had planned to scare me on purpose, it would have been a truly first-rate bit of mischief.

Which reminds me—I need to get to work on my own mischief!

Charter of the Fierce Poets Society

We hereby declare that the world is too much interested in fame and glory and money, and not enough in what really matters in life, which is poetry.

In response to that tragic fact, we now form this society, father and son against the world, dedicated to bringing truth, beauty, and enlightenment to the masses through the art of poetry, whether to be read (Bennett) or sung (Dennis).

Our motto: Verse you can trust, or your head will bust!

Our mission: Poems to brighten, enlighten, and frighten!

Our vow: To devote ourselves to poetry, no matter how we may suffer for our art!

Signed,

Dennis Carhart, songwriter

Bennett Carhart, poet

Today when little Destiny came home from school, she was sobbing as if someone had just stepped on her kitten. Mrs. Carhart was at work, of course, and Mr. C was locked away down in his Man Cave (as usual). So it was to Alex's room that the girl came.

It did my heart good to see how tender my lass was with her little sister. But what the wee girl was crying about made me fiery with anger.

"Teacher said . . . said . . . said . . ."

She was hiccuping from crying so hard, and it was difficult for her to get the words out.

"Said what?" Alex asked patiently.

"She said Herbert the Goblin wasn't real!"

Oh, my blood went aboil at hearing this. I'm pretty sure that there is no Herbert the Goblin here. (I've checked Destiny's room several times to be certain.) Even so, we of the Enchanted Realm know well and well how important a child's imagination is. The thought of Destiny's teacher squashing it this way . . . well, it was a good thing the woman wasn't in front of me at that moment. I don't think there's a number high enough for me to have counted to.

No matter how high I got bad things would likely have followed.

THRACKS TRAX MUSIC ♪ ♩ ♪
Home of Infectious Listening!
895 MELODY WAY, NASHVILLE, TN

Dear Mr. Carhart,

We recently received your collection of songs and asked one of our interns to give it a listen.

She resigned an hour later.

We must respectfully request that you please never, never, never send us any samples of your songs again.

Ever.

Sincerely,

Ann Thracks

cc: Dee Umbo

When Alex came home from soccer this afternoon, I went out to talk. After we had chatted for a bit, I said, "I want you to take me to school with you on Monday."

"Why in the world do you want to go back?" she asked. "You told me you're not supposed to be seen."

"I'm going to break that rule," I said. "I want to have a little chat with Destiny's teacher."

Alex's smile was so big, it lit up my heart. "Thank you!"

Soon we arranged that I would ride in her backpack in the morning. (She gave me a spit swear she would clean it out first.) The point of this was to get me inside the building without me having to climb the walls in search of an open window. Then at the end of the day, she would walk past Destiny's classroom and let me out nearby.

I should sleep now, but I am too excited about Monday to settle down. I wish Fergus were here so I could talk to him about this. I think what I have in mind qualifies both as a mischief and cleaning up a mess all at once, which counts as a double score. With luck, maybe even enough to cover the bad thing I am planning to do of letting myself be seen.

(When I think of the number of times I have broken the Great Oath since Sarah died, it fills me with fear and apprehension.)

FROM THE JOURNAL OF
ALEX CARHART

10/24 (Sat.)

Well, it's not journal day, but I'm writing here anyway because there's a lot on my mind.

Maybe Mrs. W was right about this.

So ... first off, big things going on with the 'rents. Mom found out that Dad's old boss offered to take him back and she is NOT HAPPY that Dad isn't going for it.

I know this because Ben and Destiny and I sat on the stairs and listened while they fought about it.

When Mom told Dad he should "come to his senses," he answered that he <u>had</u> finally come to his senses and that was why he quit to begin with.

"How are we going to pay the mortgage?" Mom said. "We'll be out on the street in six months!"

I think she was exaggerating.

I HOPE she was exaggerating.

I don't want Dad to be unhappy. He is always telling us we should follow our dreams, and I think he should be able to do the same thing.

On the other hand, I don't want to end up being an eleven-year-old bag lady!

In other news, Bennett's girlfriend broke up with him.

Turns out she didn't like his poetry.

Sunday, October 25 (evening)

Quiet day. Family all at home, so I am mostly staying inside the Pink Horror.

Alex and I have set our plans for tomorrow. It should be an interesting day.

What happened when I went to talk to Destiny's teacher today was stranger than I expected, and quite troubling.

Things started out well enough. I rode to school in Alex's pack, as we had planned. She really had cleaned it out, mostly. I see glimmers of hope for the girl. I had a wee bottle of water and some provisions, so I did not get too hungry as the day went on. To my surprise, I enjoyed listening to the things that went on in the classroom, especially when Mrs. Winterbotham was reading to the students.

In the afternoon I dozed off for a while—it was fair hot in that backpack. I woke only when Alex picked up the pack and whispered, "Here we go!"

We stopped outside Destiny's room, where the teacher was bidding the children good-bye for the afternoon. Alex set down her pack and said, "Destiny is going to walk home with me today."

"That's nice," said the teacher. Though she was all sweetness and light, I could see that the wee girl had been crying again.

While Alex and Ms. Kincaid were talking, I climbed out of the pack and scurried into the room. Fair quick I found the perfect thing for what I had in mind. On the shelf beneath the windows was a puppet of a purple dragon. I leaped up to examine the thing. It was beautifully made. Even better, it had plenty of room for a brownie to hide inside it.

I lifted the puppet's tail and slipped up its behind. A perfect fit!

Finally Ms. Kincaid came back into the room. She went to her desk and started correcting papers. I waited until she was occupied, then shoved my hands into the puppet's head and began to flap its jaws. Next I let out a roar. Then I shouted in the fiercest voice I could muster, "You were not at your best today!"

Oh, I was fair beside myself with delight at my cleverness!

Ms. Kincaid looked up, startled, and stared around the room.

"Who said that?" she called.

I stood up, bringing the puppet to a rearing position, then flapped its jaws again as I bellowed, "You were not at your best today! You made a child cry!"

The teacher leaped to her feet. I pulled my hands out of the puppet's jaw and thrust them into its armholes. Then I began to dance on the counter, waving the dragon's arms.

"What is this?" cried the teacher. "Who are you?"

She looked around wildly and I knew she was trying to spot someone playing a trick on her. So I backed out from the puppet. Once clear of it, I spread my arms and said cheerfully, "Here I am!"

Ms. Kincaid staggered back. "Who are you? *What* are you?"

"I'm Destiny's friend Herbert. The one you said doesn't exist. Oh, I know she says I'm a goblin when I'm really a brownie. But she's just a wee girl, so I'd think you could forgive her for the confusion. The question is, what excuse do you have for stomping on her imagination? What are you going to do next? Tell her Santa Claus is dead, the Easter Bunny just got served for dinner, and the Tooth Fairy is in jail for stealing molars? In which case you would be wrong, wrong, and wrong."

Ms. Kincaid put her hand to her mouth and stared at me with an expression so strange and wild it baffled me. I had expected her to be surprised, and perhaps a bit frightened. But there was something else in her face, something I could not understand.

I leaped from the counter to the floor, hurried to her desk, then bounded up onto it.

"Are you listening to me?" I demanded.

She closed her eyes, pressed her hands to her temples, and murmured, "The pressure has been too much. I've started to hallucinate."

I leaped to her shoulder, grabbed a lock of her hair, and tugged, saying, "Does that feel like a hallucination? Now listen, I have something important to tell you. I know it's hard to believe in a little girl's imagination, but if you are going to be her teacher, you need to let her have her dreams, not stomp and squash them. When you decided to become a teacher, you didn't start out to be a dream squasher, did you?"

"Of course not! I want to build dreams. But I . . . I . . ."

I heard so much pain in her voice that I felt confused. Leaping from her shoulder to the desk, I stood in front of her and said, "Listen to me, miss. Everyone has a bad day. I ought to know, having had plenty of them myself. But having a bad day does not make you a bad person. I myself have a notoriously horrible temper. Really, it's quite appalling sometimes."

She was listening, I could tell. But something else was going on, too. She reached out a hand to me. I should have backed away, but the move was slow, tentative, and I could sense that she was scared but also—and this was strange— filled with some odd sense of hope.

"May I touch you?" she asked. "Just to see if you're real? I won't hurt you, I promise."

"Will you let Destiny keep her imaginary friend?" I asked.

She nodded, then put the tip of her finger on my shoulder.

Then she fainted dead away!

At first I thought I had killed her with shock. But that made no sense, and when I checked, I could tell she was still breathing. So I went to one of those long, narrow windows and (using my brownie strength) wrenched down the handle and pulled it open.

I climbed out and went to meet Alex.

"How did it go?" she asked.

"I'll tell you when we get home," I said, still shaken.

After the Carharts were done with supper that night, Alex brought me some milk and a nice bit of tattie, though when I thanked her for it, I had to explain that "tattie" was just a word we use for potato back in Scotland.

I am often amazed that though we speak the same language, we have so many different words for things. Sometimes it makes communication quite difficult. Anyway, while I was eating we talked about my meeting with Ms. Kincaid. Alex agrees that there was something more going on than we can understand right now. I am mystified, and somewhat nervous.

CASE NOTES ON BENNETT CARHART

10/26

First meeting with BC this afternoon. He seems a nice-enough teenager, and a very intelligent one.

His mother's concern, the reason she brought him to me, is that Bennett has undergone a rapid personality change, shifting from a sports orientation to an obsession with writing. Specifically, he has recently developed an overpowering urge to write poetry.

Unfortunately, he is appallingly bad at it. He brought some of his poems with him. I was hard-pressed to maintain a professional air while reading them. The truth is, I nearly snorted coffee through my nose. They are hilariously awful!

Early diagnosis: Bennett seems to be suffering from some odd version of hypergraphia.

It is an interesting case, and I look forward to working with him.

I just hope he won't ask me to read his poems every week!

From the files of Dr. Eli Vator

Tuesday, October 27

Things are tense in the house, what with Mr. Carhart mooning and moaning down in the cellar over his horrible songs, and Bennett moaning and mooning in his room over his wretched verse, and Mrs. Carhart fretting and fussing about both of them. However, things have been getting friendlier between Alex and myself.

Alas, I fear I made a grave mistake this night and that friendliness may come to an end.

The evening started off well enough, with Alex bringing me some milk and biscuits. Only when I called them biscuits, she laughed and said they were cookies.

Despite the silly name, I quite liked the "cookies," which were chocolate with white cream inside. Perhaps not everything in this country is barbaric after all. About half of one is all I could manage, though. Even at that I felt stuffed. The things are bigger than my head!

My head

Cookie

Angus

Alex ate the other half of mine, along with four or five more.

While I was working on my half cookie, she said to me, "Angus, how did you get here from Scotland? Did you fly?"

"Do I look like I have wings?"

"No need to be snippy!"

"Sorry. It was a hard trip. I came through the Enchanted Realm."

That was the first slip, as I'm nae supposed to speak of the Realm to humans. But once it was out of my mouth, I had to explain. Between letting myself be seen by Ms. Kincaid and now this, I fear I've become a right renegade.

Well, anyway, I began to tell about my journey through the Enchanted Realm. Alex listened with wide eyes. When I got to the part about needing to cross the Shadow Sea and started to tell her about the selkie, she burst out with, "Wait! Are you telling me selkies are *real*?"

"I'm real, aren't I? Why should a selkie be any more surprising than a brownie?"

She closed her eyes and shook her head, as if trying to take this in. "Is *everything* real? I mean, all the things in the old stories? Like, oh, mermaids and goblins and trolls and . . . well, everything?"

"Oh, aye."

"Can I ever meet some?"

"Well, I don't know what sorts you have in the Enchanted Realm about here."

"You mean there's part of the Enchanted Realm here in America?" she asked, all excited.

"Oh, aye. Why should there be magic in one part of the world and not others? Sure, and it's stronger in some places, like my dear old Scotland. But there's no place totally void of it."

She looked delighted at this idea.

Then she asked the question that led me to say what I should not have.

"How did you end up bound to my family?"

"It's a long story," I replied without thinking. "And it starts long ago, with a lad named Ewan McGonagall. Why don't you go onto that intermagoogle thing you've told me about and see if you can find the tale of what happened to him?"

The moment the words left my flapping yap, I knew I had made a dreadful mistake.

Once Alex knows the story, she will also know about the curse.

She will know, too, that I have brought it with me into this house.

The Tale of Ewan McGonagall

from *Legends, Lore, and Lunacy of the Scots People*

by Jane Hyatt Stemple

Once in a Highland Village, there lived a lad who met a strange creature, and made a strange mistake, and suffered a strange fate.

His name was Ewan McGonagall, and on the day he was born, Fiona Duffy, the village wisewoman, said, "Och, he's an odd one, likely to be a burden to his mother's heart and a bane to his father's wishes."

Alas, her words proved true, for the lad was as full of mischief as a hive is full of honey. He was an ear tweaker and a pigtail puller, an ink spiller and a plate breaker. His poor mother spent hours praying for something to improve the boy, but her prayers went unanswered.

He was even more of a bother to his father, for he could no more tend a flock than a brick can darn a sock, and the best he could do with a hammer was sometimes not hit himself in the head with it.

The one thing he could do, and do well, was sing. Oh,

when he sang, busy men would stop to listen, birds would cease their warbling, and snarling dogs would come to lie silent at his feet. It was not just his voice. He had a wondrous way with words, and the songs he sang were his own, unlike any ever heard before. It was as if poetry flowed in his veins.

Even the faerie folk loved to hear Ewan sing . . . loved it a bit too much, for that was why they decided to lure him into the Enchanted Realm, which was how the trouble began.

It happened on a moonlit night, when the youth had tarried too long at a friend's. As he was homeward traipsing, he spotted a silver path wending among the trees. "That's the road for me," he said to himself, and off he started. But before he had gone very far, he heard a small voice cry, "Oh, woe! Oh, woe! Is there none who can help me?"

Looking up, he saw an owl perched on the branch of a tree. The bird was standing on one leg. Clutched in the talons of the other leg was a little man no more than a foot high. From the way the owl was looking at the man, it was clear to Ewan it would be but a moment before the poor fellow was inside the owl, rather than outside.

At once the lad began to sing about how the owl no more wanted to eat the little man than it wanted to have its wings taken away. The bird listened, and on the third verse it swooped down to drop the wee fellow at Ewan's feet, then soared off into the moonlight.

Ewan knelt to look at the little man and saw, by both his size and his clothing, that he was a brownie.

Making a bow to Ewan, the brownie said, "For saving me from that great beast, you have my gratitude, and more than that my promise to serve you when you are in need."

Ewan thought it unlikely that anyone this small could do him much good in times of trouble. Still, he was a polite lad, so he said, "I thank you for that, my wee friend. But right now I am bound on following this moonlit road to see where it may lead me."

"Straight to trouble would be my guess," said the brownie, "for this is sure a path to the Enchanted Realm, which is nae place for humanfolk."

"Still and all, I feel I must follow it," said Ewan.

"Then follow it with you will I, for my life is bound with yours."

And sure enough the path, silver in the moonlight, takes Ewan and the brownie straight to Dunloch Hill, which was well known in the village as a place not to go. And wasn't the hill open at its root? And didn't the path lead right inside, shining still even when it was well out of the moonlight? And despite all that, didn't Ewan McGonagall walk right in as if he had not an ounce of sense in his head, which most folk thought was the case anyway?

And wasn't the merriment in the hill in part because they had lured Ewan to their midst, and in part because the Queen of Shadows was there as well, dressed in black and hard to see save for the great ruby that glittered at her neck?

"There you are, Ewan McGonagall!" said the Lord of the Hill when he spotted Ewan. "We've been hoping you would visit us some moonlit night. We'll have a song if you will, and even if you won't, for there's no way you'll be leavin' without some singing first."

"There's no need to threaten," replied Ewan, "for I'm more than happy to give you a song." And straightaway he began to sing.

If words had always come easy to Ewan, they now came easier than ever. And if his voice had always been honey sweet and silk smooth, it was even more so now. Too sweet and smooth for his own good, for when he had sung seven songs, the Lord of the Hill said, "You must no more go out in the world, for we need your singing here."

"I am thankful of the compliment," Ewan answered. "But I must go back, or me ma and me da will be a worrittin' over me."

"Will you not stay for me, singer?" asked a soft voice. Then from behind the Queen of Shadows stepped her daughter, the Princess of Sunshine, who was as bright as the queen was dark, with flowing hair of gold and glowing eyes of blue.

"Nae, nae, I canna stay," said Ewan sadly, for his heart was filled with sudden longing for the girl. With the brownie still by his side, he turned and left the hill. But not all of him came home that night, for a part of his heart remained in the Enchanted Realm, held tight in the grip of the girl who had stolen it with just one glance.

After a week of sighs and moaning, Ewan said to the brownie, "I must go back to the hill."

"If you go in once more, out again you'll never come," said the brownie. "But I will take a message for you, if you wish, for I can come and go in the Enchanted Realm as I please."

So Ewan asked the brownie to tell the daughter of the Queen of Shadows that he wished to sing for her as he has never sung for anyone, would she but come to meet him. Off the brownie went with the message, leaving Ewan to swoon and swan about the town, singing such woeful songs that the flowers wilted, the birds hid their heads beneath their wings, and the cows gave naught but sour milk.

About the time the townfolk were ready to send him into the woods so they could stop crying themselves to sleep at night, the brownie returned with word that the Princess of Sunshine was pining with love for Ewan, just as he was pining for her, but she could not come to him, for her mother had locked her away.

Now Ewan's songs were sweet but melancholy, for he was filled with joy at the thought that she loved him, but sadder than ever that they were apart and he could not feed her words of gold.

At last he went to the village schoolmaster and asked the old man to write down his words. Then he sang a song so sweet and sad that the teacher's eyes dropped tears upon the paper as he wrote.

The gift of the poem ready, once more the brownie carried the message into the hill.

Long was he gone, and the longer he tarried, the more Ewan's heart was wrung within him. What had happened? What was happening?

Just when Ewan thought he could bear the waiting no more, the brownie reappeared, carrying a note from the Princess of Sunshine.

Now for many a month did this go on, with the brownie taking messages back and forth, back and forth. And with each message both the joy and the sorrow of the young lovers was heightened. Finally one day the brownie came to Ewan and said, "The Queen of Shadows wishes to see you. Though I would advise you against going once more into the hill, I have no choice but to deliver this message."

"Into the hill I go!" replied Ewan without a second's thought.

So that night the brownie led him back to Dunloch Hill. Once inside, Ewan found the Queen of Shadows waiting with her daughter, who was now little more than a shadow herself.

"Ewan McGonagall!" said the queen, her eyes ablaze and her voice fierce as bee stings. "We made a mistake by inviting you into our world, that I know now. But you have made a greater mistake in not leaving it be. Had you bid us farewell and nevermore tampered here, things might yet have been well. But with the help of this interfering brownie, you have wrought great damage. Now my child, who is the light of my life, is losing light herself. So tonight I give you a choice. You may take my daughter to be your wife, if in return you surrender your greatest gift as bride price."

"Oh, Mother, no!" gasped the fairy girl.

But the queen ignored her and said, "Tell me, Ewan McGonagall, for I need to know the extent of your love. What shall it be, my daughter or your singing?"

Ewan did not hesitate but said at once, "Your daughter is worth all the songs that ever were or ever will be."

"Then she is yours," said the queen. "But in taking her from my side, you and that brownie both earn my curse. And the curse I lay upon you, Ewan McGonagall, will echo through your generations. And the curse I lay upon this wretched brownie is to be the bearer of that curse. He shall be bound to you and your descendants until the day one of them returns to me that which you have stolen, and will carry the curse with him into each home he enters."

With that, the queen released her daughter, who ran to Ewan's arms. And though the girl sorrowed much that

he could no longer sing, she knew his heart from the songs she had heard already, and knew it was that heart that she had come to love.

So the two of them, the human lad and the fairy girl, loved together for long and long, though he grew old and she did not. And they had a daughter, radiant as the sun, but with the voice of a crow.

When the time came for Ewan to leave this earth, he did so willingly, feeling he had lived long and well. But the Princess of Sunshine, unwilling to return to the Enchanted Realm, began to wander, and wanders still for all I know.

And that is the tale of Ewan McGonagall.

"Angus Cairns, I want to talk to you!"

These were the first words out of Alex's mouth as she slammed into the room this afternoon.

She sounded quite like her mother.

I had no need to ask what she wanted to talk about, for I had been dreading this moment since I opened my haggis hole and told her to look up the story of Ewan McGonagall.

"Come out here! Right now!"

I crept from the Pink Horror.

She stared down at me, hands on her hips, and said, "The brownie in the story is you, right?"

"No, not me. It was my da."

"All right, it was your father. But you're the one who carries the curse now, right?"

I lowered my head. "I had hoped it was over," I mumbled.

"Why would you hope that if you're still bound by the stupid thing yourself?"

"Because it's been nearly a hundred years since the Curse of the McGonagalls has struck. And it has never struck in a house where I served."

"And why is that?"

"It only strikes the men of the line, and in the time since I became Curse Bearer, I have never been assigned to a house with a man in it. Also, some magic can't cross the water."

I realized how weak that last sounded even as I said it.

"So what, exactly, is this curse?"

"Wait here," I said.

"Where are you going?"

"Just into the Pink Horror to get something. I'll be right out."

When I returned, Alex was sitting at her desk. I could almost see rays of anger shooting out of her head.

"Get up here," she demanded, pointing to the desk.

I scrambled up.

"What have you got?"

I handed her a scroll of parchment. "Here it is—the curse itself."

She made a face. "I can't read something that tiny."

"Just take it!"

She held out her hand and I dropped the scroll into her palm. The minute it landed, it began to grow. She yelped in surprise but didn't move.

When it stopped growing, I said, "Take off the ribbon and read for yourself."

Then I braced myself for what was to follow.

The Curse of the McGonagalls

Now do I, Greer M'Greer, Queen of Scotland's Enchanted Realm, lay this curse upon Ewan McGonagall and the men of all the generations of his line that shall follow.

You shall long to be poets. Your hearts shall burn with a fierce desire for words that take wing, phrases that lift the spirit, and verse that stirs the soul. But until the day you or one of your descent makes good for the cruel pain you have wrought against me with your till-now silver tongue, never shall fair line of verse, nor pleasing rhyme, nor elegant phrase pass your lips nor flow from your pen. Until all is made right, you shall be plagued with thoughts of gold that escape as words of lead. Your poetry shall be as the braying of asses, your rhymes a discordant clanging that assaults the ear when heard and affronts the eye when read. Your dearest thoughts, when expressed in any but the simplest terms, shall bring naught but mock and jest.

And all this I declare but fair punishment for the way you used your silver tongue and sweet words to do the wrong you've done me. And only when what is now lost by me to a McGonagall male is returned to me by a male of the same line shall this curse be lifted.

So say I, Greer M'Greer, Queen of Shadows.

And so shall it be!

Alex put down the paper and stared at me in horror. Then she whispered, "You're the reason Dad quit his job, aren't you?"

I hung my head.

"And why Bennett is writing ghastly poems and moping around like a lovesick loon."

"Aye, that would be my fault, too."

"Angus, you can't stay. You just can't!"

I nodded. "I understand. I'll pack my things and wait until it's dark. Then I'll go."

"Can you really do that? You kept telling me you had no choice."

"I don't know. I've never tried to leave a home before."

"Well, you left to bring that report to me at school."

"Yes, but I was planning to come back. This is different. I'll be trying to leave forever."

Alex nodded and said, "I'll walk with you when you go." She sounded a bit sad, which touched me at the heart.

As for me, I am filled with frets and terror. I have packed my things, such as they are. I even went to say good-bye to the cat.

Now I can do naught but sit and wait.

In an hour I will leave, or at least try to.

I know not what will happen.

FROM THE JOURNAL OF
ALEX CARHART

10/29 (Thurs.)

I'm afraid Angus is dying!

It was so horrible what happened when he tried to leave last night. Now I don't know what to do. It's not like I can take him to a doctor or anything.

He's still breathing, so that's good, but I can't wake him up. I'm so scared!

This is the first time I have felt strong enough to write since my failed attempt to leave.

It was bad, even worse than I had feared.

Here is what happened. Half an hour after it grew dark, Alex said to her mother, "I need to go to Tiana's to do our homework—it's a team thing."

Mrs. Carhart made a bit of a fuss, but Alex talked her into it. It was cool outside, so she wore her big coat.

I was tucked inside one of the pockets.

Tiana's house is behind Alex's, so we left through the back door. As soon as we were outside, Alex lifted me out of her pocket.

She was true to her promise to walk with me. It was a good thing she did. Indeed, I don't know what would have happened if she hadn't, since as we drew close to the edge of the Carharts' yard, a horrid chill seized me. After a few more steps something began to churn within me. My stomach grew sick and woozy. My heart felt like a knife was twisting in it. I began to gasp for breath, but the air burned my lungs.

"What's wrong?" Alex asked.

"It's the curse, trying to keep me from going!"

Though I was shaky, I continued to walk, hoping that

if I made it past the property line, the worst would be over. Soon my legs were trembling so fiercely I could hardly stand. I felt as if a great hand, bigger and stronger than Bennett's, was squeezing me about the middle.

The churning in my stomach grew more intense. I fell to my knees and vomited out the farewell cookie Alex had shared with me before we left the house.

"Angus?"

"We'll keep going," I wheezed, pushing myself back up.

But we didn't keep going much longer. A black haze swam before my eyes. Fire seemed to run in my veins.

I let out a little scream.

That was the last I knew until I woke to find myself back in my shoe box inside the Pink Horror.

It's day now, so Alex is at school. I do not know how much time has gone by.

Nor do I know what she will have to say to me when she gets home.

I do know that I am not looking forward to it.

I would go out and clean, but I am too weak.

I am even missing Halloween, the most important day of the year in the Enchanted Realm.

Must sleep more now.

FROM THE JOURNAL OF ALEX CARHART

10/31 (Sat.)

Angus has recovered! Really, I was terrified that he was going to die. But now I don't know what to do. He can't stay here. I can't let him. Mom is ready to kill Dad as it is, and Dad is going nuts from trying to write beautiful songs, which he is totally unable to do. Last night he came up to sing me a new one and I had to tell him that rhyming "focus" with "mucus" was a bad idea, especially in a love song.

He looked so sad I thought he was going to cry. I think he really believed it was brilliant. The curse seems to have hit him even harder than it hit Bennett. Maybe it's because he's older.

I need to ask Angus if people ever get used to it. They must, or they would just end up flinging themselves off bridges or something. But even if they do get used to it, they must be so sad.

Well, I can't ask him now. He's sleeping again, which is what he has mostly been doing for the last couple of days. I'm so worried about him I'm not even going out trick-or-treating tonight. I feel like I need to be here in case he needs me.

And what am I going to do about him? I suppose we could try leaving again, and when we got to the point where he collapsed, I could pick him up and throw him into the next yard. But I'm afraid that might kill him. Or some dog or owl or something might come along and eat him.

I think I'm going to be sick.

Sunday, November 1

Last night I tested my theory that I could leave the Carhart property as long as I was planning to come back.

I'm happy to say that it worked.

The reason I left was so I could return to the Enchanted Realm and try to find Weegun. I needed someone from the Realm to talk to, to see if I could figure out a way to break this cursed curse.

I explained my plan to Alex, then asked if she could direct me to the nearest kirk. She looked at me oddly and said, "We don't have any Kirks in our class."

"Well, no, you wouldna have one in your class. It wouldna fit."

"What are you talking about?" she asked.

"What are *you* talking about?" I replied.

We have a lot of conversations like this. Fortunately, we are getting better at working them out. Before things got too cranky, we managed to figure out that what I call a kirk, she calls a church.

"Why do you want to find a church?" she asked when we had things clear.

"I must go three times round it widdershins to get back into the Enchanted Realm."

Then I had to explain widdershins, of course.

Well, no need to talk more about that, or the trip to the kirk, other than to say that I was right about the curse. Being pure in my intent of returning this time, I felt no disturbance in my guts as I left. What a difference from the other night!

I didn't know how I was to find Weegun once I was back in the Realm, but that turned out to be easily managed as well, for I had not been there even an hour when he came strolling towards me. When I asked him how he knew I had come, he said, "We've set many a spell to protect our borders, Angus Cairns. I knew the moment you returned to the Enchanted Realm, just as I knew the first day that you entered our territory and came to greet you. You didn't really think that was a coincidence, did you?"

Though he didn't say it, I was fair sure he also meant that he had come to make sure I was up to no mischief.

When I told him of my problem, he said, "Alas, that is not something I can help with. But maybe Granny Squannit can give you some advice."

"And who is Granny Squannit?"

"The oldest and wisest of all the Makiaweesug. Come, I'll take you to her. It would be better if you had a gift for her, but as you did not know you were going to see her, it may be all right."

It was a lengthy walk, and finally Weegun asked if I

would like to ride on his shoulder. Normally I would prefer to stay on my own two feet, but as I wanted to be back before dawn, I accepted his offer.

At last we came to an opening in the side of a hill. Within the hill, the halls were lit by torches that made no smoke. We twisted and turned through tunnels till we came to a chamber that had a fire blazing in its center. This fire did smoke, but the smoke rose straight to a hole in the rocky roof, and passed from there into the night.

On the far side of the fire sat a woman whose long white hair hung over her face. She rose when we entered. Though she was no taller than Weegun, she was at least twice as wide.

"Who is that riding on your shoulder, Weegun?" she asked.

I shivered, for I knew by her voice that I was in the presence of one of the ancient ones.

"He is Angus Cairns, and of the Enchanted Realm," Weegun answered. "He came from across the Shadow Sea."

"Did he come on the trading ships?"

I near fell off Weegun's shoulder at that question. Why did no one tell me there were trading ships on the Shadow Sea? I would far rather have come here on one of those than by selkie!

"I will let him tell his story in his own words," said

Weegun as he plucked me from his shoulder and placed me on the floor.

"Come to my side of the fire, small one," the woman ordered.

I did as she asked, eager to draw close to her, but at the same time frightened by the great power I sensed in her.

"Tell me your story," she said.

"That could take all of the night," I replied.

She chuckled. "We have time enough. As you well know, or at least ought to, time passes differently here in the Enchanted Realm, sometimes faster than in the human world, sometimes slower. I will make this a slow night. Speak as if you have all the time in the world."

So I told her everything, from the time my da met Ewan McGonagall, up to the problem that had brought me to her this night. If she lost patience or thought a part unimportant, she waved her hand, and I would hurry past it. Other times she held her hand palm out, signaling me to slow down. Then I would speak in more detail.

As we were outside of regular time, I have no idea how long it took me to tell her all this.

When I finished, she said, "That is quite a tale, Angus Cairns. And you have come to me because you wish to find a way to break the curse, is that right?"

I nodded, my mouth so dry from talking I was not sure I could squeeze out another word.

"Speak up," she ordered.

"Yes," I said huskily. "I do not wish to bring such grief and problems to the house where I am now bound."

"How did your father deal with such things?"

I had wondered about this myself, and only half understood. "I think it may have been different in Scotland. Back there we expect life to be dour, and things to be hard, and a curse like this would be but one more hardship. Here . . . I don't know. Somehow it seems as if these Americans feel they are in control of their destiny and can make things work out, and when they canna, it hits them harder than it ever would have on the old home soil."

At this the old woman laughed. "I do think you've put a finger on it, Angus Cairns. I do think you've put a finger on it. Now listen to me. This curse will not be easy to break. I know the Queen of Shadows, and she is not one to let go of anger easily. The only thing you can do is follow the terms of the curse and return to her what has been lost."

"How can I do that?"

Stroking a lock of her hair, Granny Squannit said slowly, "The answer may be closer at hand than you think. Magical things tend to draw together. But you'll have to open your eyes and ask questions. Beyond that, I cannot say, other than to tell you that if you do find what was lost, you must go back to Scotland to return it. And not you alone, of course. If you've properly told me the curse, a male of the McGonagall line must do the actual returning."

My heart quailed at the memory of my last crossing. "You spoke of trading ships," I said. "Are there really such things?"

"Oh, of course. Great silvery ships that ply the Shadow Sea. They ride on ghost winds and make the transport smoother than ever it could be on the seas of the human world. But they will not take on passengers for free. There will be a price. There is always a price."

"And what will it be?" I asked.

"That depends on the captain. Each can set his own fare. I should warn you, they can be quite whimsical about it."

I bowed. "Thank you. You have not solved my troubles, but—"

She interrupted me. "No, I have not, nor can I. That is up to you, Angus Cairns."

"You have not solved my troubles," I repeated. "But you have given me hope, and that is no small thing."

"Hard to say whether I have given you hope, or you are simply catching it from the hope-befuddled humans who live on this side of the Shadow Sea. However, I will give you something else, something solid that may be of use. It would be a sad thing were you to go back to break the curse, only to find that ten years or more had gone by in the human world while you were in the Enchanted Realm. So I have a gift for you. Think of it as return for the strange and interesting story you gave me this night."

She began to rummage beneath that curtain of white hair. After a moment, she extended a plump hand.

In it was a wooden peg.

"Take it," she ordered.

"Thank you," I said, accepting the piece of wood. "What is it?"

"A time peg. If you do make the trip to the far side of the Shadow Sea, it will be of great use to you. Simply pound it into the ground at the spot where you enter the Realm. The peg will lock you to that time, and as long as no one removes it, you will be able to come back to the human world at the exact moment you left."

"Oh, this is a great gift indeed! What can I do in return?"

"Come back and tell me your story when all is said and done, and all is done and said. I wish to know how you make out."

"That I will do, and gladly," I said.

"Then go now," she said, waving a hand. "It is late, and

I grow weary. Weegun will accompany you to the place where you must reenter the human world."

I bowed again, then followed Weegun out of the stony hill.

As we walked, he spoke to me of the ships that ply the Shadow Sea. There is so much of the world that I know so little of. How can I be well over a hundred years old and still feel such an infant?

FROM THE JOURNAL OF
ALEX CARHART

11/1 (Sun.)

When I got up this morning, I peeked in the dollhouse and saw that Angus had made it back from his trip. He's sound asleep now, and I don't want to wake him. So it's a good time to catch up on my journal. The main thing to report is that Dad has pretty much locked himself in his studio, except when he comes up to sing us another new song. They're getting worse.

He and Bennett have formed some kind of Dread Poets Society. They read their stuff to each other and then congratulate each other on how good it is.

Great. The last thing either of them needs is reinforcement!

Seriously, how can anyone write a poem like:

I'm starting to lose focus
And my heart feels like a crocus
But when you tear my petals off
I feel so sad I want to cough!

What the heck does "I feel so sad I want to cough!" even mean?

No wonder Bennett's jock friends have started to tease him.

I could throttle Angus for this, except I know it's not really his fault (though it feels like it is). Besides, I'm afraid that if I did throttle him, the curse would still be in effect, and I need him to help get rid of the thing!

My stomach hurts most of the time now.

Also, I'm not sleeping very well. Friday I got yelled at for nodding off at my desk.

This afternoon I reported to Alex everything that happened on my trip to the Enchanted Realm. She was both excited and horrified.

"We've got to do something soon," she said. "There are only a few days left for Dad to get his job back. If we can't break the curse before that time runs out, my family is in big trouble."

"Well, how are we to do that? We would have to return what's been lost to the queen, and we can't do that because we don't have it!"

"What, exactly, has been lost?" Alex asked. "Get out the curse again. Let's read it carefully."

I did as she asked. When we were done studying it, she groaned and said, "If I'm right, what was lost is the queen's daughter."

"Aye. And we've no idea where she is, or even if she's still alive. And even if we did, it wouldn't do any good for me to take her back. It would have to be your brother or your father."

Alex laughed at this.

"What's so funny?" I asked.

"I was just thinking of Dad going to the Enchanted Realm."

I smiled at that, but it was not enough to lift me out of the glums. Though I didn't want to come here, these Carharts are good people and I've grown fond of them, even Bennett the lout. I wanted to do as I ought, and keep their house trim and fair.

Instead I have brought shame and ruin upon them.

The oddest thing happened today. When the children arrived home from school, Destiny came into Alex's room. This was before I had come out to speak to Alex, so I watched through one of the windows of the Pink Horror.

The wee girl had with her a tiny envelope, about an inch and a half long. She handed it to Alex, who looked at it and scowled. "This says it's for 'Herbert the Brownie.' I thought Herbert was a goblin."

Destiny shook her head. "Teacher says he's really a brownie, but she's a little mixed up. Anyway, this isn't for Herbert. It's for the brownie."

"Then why are you giving it to me?" Alex asked cautiously.

"'Cause you have a brownie living in your room."

"What makes you say that?" asked Alex, and I felt a bit of warmth towards her because I saw she was trying to keep me secret.

"I seen him," Destiny said.

Clearly I had not been as cautious as I thought! Ah, weel. 'Tis nae so bad to be seen by a wee one as by an adult. And as I had already violated the Great Oath by showing myself to Destiny's teacher, the worst of the harm was done already.

"Well, give it to me and I'll make sure that he gets it," Alex said.

Destiny shook her head. "Teacher asked me to give it to him myself."

At that, I came out of the Pink Horror.

Alex gasped when she saw me, but Destiny smiled and said, "See, I knew he was real!"

Then she handed me the envelope.

Printed on the front, in tiny handwriting, was *Herbert the Brownie.*

Clearly the first thing I needed to do was get this name thing straightened out.

"Well, go on! Open it!" said Alex.

I ripped open the envelope.

Inside was a carefully folded piece of paper.

I took it out and unfolded it.

"What does it say?" Alex demanded.

Trembling a bit, I handed it to her.

I need to see you again.
Please come tomorrow.
Very important!
—Lorna Kincaid

After Alex read the note, I said, "What do you think I should do?"

"I don't know. You don't think she's some kind of brownie bounty hunter, do you?"

Destiny spoke up. "Ms. Kincaid was very nice to me today. She said she was sorry for not believing me about Herbert."

"Actually, my name is Angus."

"Well, I know you're not Herbert, silly. He's a goblin!"

"Do you want me to take you to school with me tomorrow?" asked Alex.

"I think I should go. But I don't want to spend the day in your backpack. I'll ask Bubbles if he's willing to give me a ride."

Alex looked at me in amazement. "Bubbles lets you ride him?"

"Yes, but don't say anything about it in front of him. He finds it embarrassing. Anyway, if he will bring me in the afternoon, you can meet me outside when school lets out, then carry me back in."

"All right, it's a plan. But I think I should come to see Ms. Kincaid with you, just in case."

"In case what?"

"In case she has any mischief in mind! You may be an awful pain, but I have no intention of letting her capture you or anything."

"I'll take that as a compliment, sort of."

She smiled. "It *was* a compliment, sort of."

I should be sleeping now, but I am deep in the frets, wondering what this is about and what will happen tomorrow.

Things have gotten very strange.

I went to the school this afternoon as planned. (Bubbles was quite good about agreeing to carry me, and Alex got me in with no problem.)

When we entered Ms. Kincaid's room, she looked surprised to see Alex. I caught this, because I was peeping out of the top of the backpack.

When a teacher is more surprised to see a student than to see what she must have thought until the day before was a mythical person, things have truly gone upside down!

In answer to Ms. Kincaid's expression, Alex said firmly, "I'm the chaperone."

The teacher nodded, then whispered, "Have you brought the . . . other one . . . with you?"

Alex set the backpack on one of the tables, and out I climbed.

I had hoped for this meeting with Ms. Kincaid to be more cordial than our first. To my dismay, she burst into tears again!

"Here, now, why are you crying? I'm nae here to talk fierce to you. I came at your request, remember."

"It's just that . . . you're *real*!"

"Aye, I am that. But you've already seen me once, so that should be no surprise."

"You don't understand. I have someone who needs to meet you."

"And who might that be?" I asked, wary at the idea of revealing myself to yet another human.

"My great-grandmother, Ailsa McGonagall."

I near fell off the table at those words! Alex started with surprise as well.

"Where is this great-grandmother of yours, and why does she need to meet me?" I asked.

"She lives at the Happy Oaks Senior Home."

"I know her!" Alex cried. "She's my mother's favorite resident."

Ms. Kincaid smiled. "Yes, I often see your mother when I visit Gran."

"But why does your gran need to see Angus?"

Ms. Kincaid looked puzzled. "I thought his name was Herbert," she said.

"I prefer Angus," I said quickly, not wanting to get into the whole story. "And I still want to know why your Gran needs to meet me."

Ms. Kincaid had the gift of smiling and looking sad at the same time. "Gran is very old. I don't think she has long to live. For the last couple of years, she's been talking to me about a place she calls the Enchanted Realm. And about brownies. I think it's all kind of jumbled together in her head from old stories she's remembering. Whatever the reason, it's become an obsession with her. She's sad all the time, and I know it would lift her heart if she could meet him."

"You know I'm nae supposed to be seen by humans," I said.

"But I've seen you!"

"I was taking a chance when I came to you, but I felt it was important for Destiny's sake. But I'm piling up violations of the Great Oath. The queen alone knows what price I'll pay for it someday."

"If you do this, you would make an old woman very happy."

"Will she blab about it?" Alex asked.

It made me happy to see that my girl was looking out for me.

Ms. Kincaid smiled again. "Probably. But you needn't worry about that. She talks about brownies and the old country all the time. No one will think anything of it."

I sighed. "All right, I'll come."

Writing this now, I can't help but wonder what I've gotten myself into. I would say that I am getting soft in my old age, only I'm still fair young for a brownie.

I think it must be that this new world is making me a bit mad.

That's me. A mad brownie.

Last night Alex convinced her mother that she, Alex, needed to go to Happy Oaks this afternoon so she could do a report on her mother's workplace.

"I told her it was a make-up assignment, so I could improve my grades from all the assignments I didn't hand in on time," she told me.

"Won't she wonder when your grade doesn't go up?" I asked.

She smiled. "But it will go up. I already talked Mrs. Winterbotham into letting me do it."

I'll give the girl this: when she actually wants to get something done, she can be quite determined.

When she got home today, she once again emptied her backpack onto the bed. It's nae such a problem now that I've got the thing organized. Also, I scrubbed out the inside so it's not disgusting when I ride in it.

After I had climbed inside, Alex strapped the pack to her back. Then she went to the garage and got out her bicycle.

The trip to her mother's workplace took about fifteen minutes. When we went in, I heard (from inside the back-pack) a woman tell Alex, "Your mom's waiting for you in her office, dear."

I felt a bit of a thump when Alex set her pack down on one of the chairs.

Sometimes I wish I had a wee clock to wear about my wrist as the humans do, save that I never want to worry about time that much. Still, I couldn't help but fret as I waited for what was to happen next. Finally someone picked up the pack again. Hoping it was the right person, I suddenly wondered if our plan was more foolish than I had thought.

A few minutes later, the pack was set down again. Big hands, much bigger than Alex's, opened the top, and I blinked as the light streamed in. Then I heard Ms. Kincaid say, "Thank you for coming, Angus. Shall I lift you out?"

"No, please, ma'am. I don't like to be picked up. Just lay the pack sideways and I'll come out on my own."

She did, and I crawled out. As I stood and stretched, I heard a gasp from my right. Turning, I found myself facing the oldest woman I had ever seen. Two bright blue eyes peered at me from a collection of wrinkles topped by a swirl of snow-white hair. Tears began to roll down her cheeks, but they were lost in the creases of her face, which was split in the most beautiful smile I had ever seen.

"You see, Lorna," she croaked in a dry husky voice. "I told you brownies are real."

Though her voice was harsh, to hear those words spoken as they would have been in Scotland, with the proper rise and fall and burr, was a kind of music to my ears.

Ms. Kincaid smiled. "Yes, Gran, you did indeed."

"But you didn't believe me. You should always listen to your old gran, my dear."

"Yes, you've told me that, too," said Ms. Kincaid, her voice warm with love.

"What is your name, brownie?" the old woman asked.

"Angus," I said.

"Ah. And do you have a home to care for?"

Before I could answer, there was a knock at the door.

"Who is it?" called Ms. Kincaid as I scurried under the bed.

"Alex!"

The door opened and in stepped my girl. I came out from under the bed and climbed back to where I had been standing. "I do indeed have a home to care for," I said. "It is with this fine girl, who I think you know."

I thought it best not to bother the old woman with what was happening there now due to the curse.

"You're a lucky girl, to have a brownie in your home," said the old lady.

I fear I smirked a bit at this, though I tried not to let Alex see it.

The old lady sighed and murmured, "Ah, how I long for the old country." The next thing she said sent lightning shooting through me. "How I long to return to the Enchanted Realm."

She began to weep, and soon had wept herself to sleep.

"Angus, what *is* the Enchanted Realm?" Ms. Kincaid asked.

"I'm nae allowed to speak of it."

"That might make sense if I didn't know it exists and didn't know that brownies are real. But I do. So you might as well tell me."

I sighed. "It's the world where the fair folk reside."

Ms. Kincaid squeezed her eyes shut. "I was brought up on those tales. Only my mother insisted they were real. She drove me half crazy with it, and I thought she was daft. That's why I was so hard on Destiny about her 'invisible friend.' It was so confusing to me as a child that I thought it was bad for her to be so wrapped up in it. I really am sorry for that."

"Well, all's mended on that front," I said. "But why in the world did your gran say she wants to go *back* to the Enchanted Realm?"

Ms. Kincaid shook her head. "I don't know. But, then, there's a lot about her that I don't know."

I asked what she meant, but she tightened her lips and said she had better not say anymore.

I had to count to 748 in order to avoid pitching a fit at her.

Fit or not, it's clear Lorna Kincaid knows something that she's not telling us, and we need to get it out of her.

Text messages between Alex Carhart and Lorna Kincaid

Alex
We need to talk. When can we meet?

Ms. Kincaid
I am not comfortable doing so at school. Can you come up with a reason to visit my gran at Happy Oaks again?

Alex
I can interview her for some research I'm doing on the McGonagall family.

Ms. Kincaid
Perfect! And I can say I need to be there to watch over Ailsa and make sure she doesn't get overtired. That work for you?

Alex
What time?

Ms. Kincaid
Afternoon, unless evening is better for you?

Alex
Evening. I'm mostly supposed to be keeping an eye on Destiny in the afternoon.

Ms. Kincaid
7:30?

Alex
Perfect.

Ms. Kincaid
Bring Angus?

Alex
Of course!

This morning Alex said, "We need to go back to Happy Oaks. We have to learn more about Ailsa McGonagall."

As I agreed completely, this was nae a problem, though I am getting a bit tired o' traveling around in that backpack. This time I plan to bring provisions, so I can have a wee snack while I'm stuck inside the thing.

It should be an interesting night.

11/5

To Whom It May Concern:

Alex Carhart has my permission to interview my great-grandmother, Ailsa McGonagall, in her room at Happy Oaks. This is in relation to a project Alex is working on for school.

I will be present to monitor things, and to make sure that my great-grandmother does not become fatigued.

Sincerely,

Lorna Kincaid

I will never forget this night as long as I live.

Ms. Kincaid was already in Ailsa's room when Alex arrived (with me in her backpack, of course).

Ms. Kincaid looked glad to see us, but it was her gran who was really pleased. "You've come back!" she cried as Alex entered. "Did you bring Angus?"

"Of course," Alex said. She opened the pack and out I popped.

"Come sit beside me," said Ailsa, patting the arm of her wheelchair.

I scrambled up, glad to do so.

Alex took out a notepad. "Can we ask you some questions, Mrs. McGonagall?"

The old woman stiffened, and it was as if she had pulled a curtain across the room, separating herself from Alex and me.

"It's all right, Gran," said Ms. Kincaid gently. "We're in this together now. After all, you know there's a brownie here with Alex."

"Wouldna do me a bit o' good to speak the truth," said the old woman bitterly. "There's none who would believe me."

Ms. Kincaid looked down. "I know that included me

until now, Gran, and I'm sorry. But it was too much to take in. Besides, I was trying not to believe it about myself."

That caught both Alex and me. "What do you mean, about yourself?" said Alex.

Ms. Kincaid took a deep breath, then said, "How old do you think I am?"

Alex made a face. "That is almost always a trick question."

Ms. Kincaid laughed. "Feel free to give an honest answer. I promise not to be insulted."

"Okay, from what I've heard, you're fairly new to teaching. Even so, I think you look a little old for that. So I'll say you're thirty."

"And very kind of you it is to say that to a woman who's sixty-five," said Ms. Kincaid.

Alex slid off her chair and onto the floor.

"It's a thing in the family," Ms. Kincaid said. "We just don't age the way other people do. Gran here most of all." She went to the door, opened it to make sure no one was listening, then closed it tight and came back to where we were sitting. In a low voice, she said, "Gran's papers are faked. We paid a lot of money—and dealt with some pretty unsavory people—to get them. But it was the only way to get her into Happy Oaks." She paused, then said, "I have false papers, too."

My insides were jumping as if I'd swallowed a rabbit.

Tugging on Ailsa's sleeve, I said, "Have you ever heard tell of the Princess of Sunshine?"

She closed her eyes. A slow smile spread across her face. "Ah," she murmured, "it's been many a year since anyone called me by that name. Too long. Too long. Oh, Angus, I want to go home now. It's been too long."

"Bingo!" whispered Alex.

Ms. Kincaid stared at us in astonishment.

Then she began to cry.

She's rather a soggy woman.

"What's the matter?" Alex asked.

"I've spent my life trying to pretend it wasn't true," sniffed Ms. Kincaid. "I knew my family was different, but I didn't know how different. How different am I? *What* am I, exactly?" She put her face in her hands. When she looked up again, she was a fair mess, her makeup streaked from the tears. "I made life so hard on Gran, not believing her stories."

"How did she end up in America?" asked Alex.

"That I don't know," said Ms. Kincaid.

Ailsa's eyes were closed, but she murmured, "I always tried to stay close to the family. When the last branch moved to the States, I came, too. Always felt a need to watch over them."

I looked at the lines in her face and thought about the fact that she had been aging over these three centuries, aging slowly, so very slowly, but steadily. It must have been the effect of living in the human world, rather than the Enchanted Realm, where she belonged. Could she ever die here? Or would she just keep getting older and older forever?

The thought gave me the shivers.

"I want to go home," she said again.

"It's not that simple, Gran. I can't just take you out of here and not bring you back. I'd be charged with murder!"

"You could stay in the Enchanted Realm," Ailsa whispered.

Ms. Kincaid shook her head. "What am I, one quarter of that blood? One eighth? There's no guarantee they'd have me. And I'm not at all sure I would feel comfortable there."

"Well," said Alex, "there's only one answer."

When we all looked at her, she smiled and said, "Jailbreak!"

By which I knew she meant we were going to have to steal Ailsa away from Happy Oaks in a way that could not be connected with us.

"There's one other problem," I said.

"What's that?" Alex asked.

"Bennett."

Her eyes widened as she realized what I meant. The curse was very specific. What had been taken by Ewan McGonagall must be returned by a male of direct descent.

Of course Mr. Carhart would do as well as Bennett, but Alex and I both knew the odds of getting that to happen were slim.

I didn't mention the other possible problem, which was this: What if the queen no longer *wanted* her daughter back? She had lived three hundred years in the human world and was frail and wrinkled, nothing like the Princess of Sunshine must once have been.

What would it be like for the aged princess to come home to a mother who was still young and beautiful, while she was now a crone?

This afternoon, before Mrs. Carhart was home, Alex called an emergency council of the siblings. She wasn't much worried about Mr. Carhart hearing it. He rarely comes up from his studio these days, and since the stairs creak, we would hear him coming if he did by chance rise from the depths.

I was present, though not visible, as Alex had asked me to wait in a box. It was a bit undignified, but we both knew we needed to break this to Bennett slowly.

When all three siblings were at the dining room table, Bennett said, "Can we make this quick, Al? I want to get back to my writing."

She cleared her throat, then said, "Have you noticed that things have been kind of weird around here lately?"

Bennett snorted. "You're not kidding."

"Do you want to know why?"

"Yeah. Dad has lost his mind."

It was interesting that the boy could spot his father's obsession but not his own madness. 'Tis a subtle curse indeed.

"Well, do you want to know *why* Dad has lost his mind?"

I didn't like Alex phrasing it that way, since it pretty

much meant I was the reason for this mess. But then, my presence really *was* the reason for it. So I guess it was fair.

"He's having a midlife crisis," Bennett said.

"If only it were that simple," Alex replied.

Then she picked up the box with me in it and set it on the table.

"What do you have in there?" Bennett asked.

"Brace yourself," Alex said. Then she opened the box and said, "Come on out, Angus."

I clambered over the edge and stood on the table.

Bennett shrieked and pushed his chair back so violently that it tipped over and sent him sprawling on the floor.

Destiny giggled.

"What is that thing?" cried Bennett.

Well, that set me off. Leaping near a foot into the air, I shouted, "I am nae a 'thing'! I am a brownie, a brownie fierce and proud, you great lumbering penner of putrid poetry."

I was on the edge of a real fit, but Alex put a finger on my shoulder and whispered, "Careful, Angus."

I pulled myself back. Once I did, I felt right ashamed. The poetry was my fault, not Bennett's, so it was cruel to taunt him for it.

"I'm sorry," I said. "I didna mean to say all that. But 'twas not nice to call me a thing. I'm a brownie, as I said. Not only that, I'm the brownie attached to your family."

Bennett was smacking the base of his palm against his

head. Looking at Alex, he said, "Isn't that the doll I picked up in your room a week or so ago?"

"Well, he was pretending to be a doll. He's taking a big risk by letting you see him now, Ben, since it's against brownie rules. But we've got a huge problem, and we need to work together to solve it."

"If you mean the problem of Dad quitting his job, what are we supposed to do about it?" he said, picking up his chair.

He resumed his seat, never taking his eyes from me as he moved. I was not sure whether he feared I was going to disappear or thought I might attack him.

His question brought us to the uncomfortable point, because now I had to explain about the curse. As I talked, I could see the boy getting angrier and angrier. Worse, I could hardly blame him.

"It's not his fault, Ben," Alex put in. "The whole thing goes back to some ancestor of ours. Angus is trapped in it just like you and Dad."

"I repeat: what are we supposed to do about it?"

Alex and I had prepared for this. I had the curse with me, and I handed it to him. When it started to expand in his hand, he started back but managed not to fall over again.

"Read it," said Alex.

"Read it aloud!" demanded Destiny. "I want to hear it, too."

He did as she asked. It was the first time I had heard the queen's words spoken aloud, and they chilled me anew.

When Bennett was done, he said, "I don't understand. To begin with, we're Carharts, not McGonagalls."

"Yer of the line," I said. "Descendants of Ewan's first cousin, actually. It's just that in your branch, the name was lost to marriage a generation or so back."

"All right, so we're McGonagalls. But this says that a McGonagall male has to return what was taken. I take it you expect me to do this. But as near as I can make out, what was taken was this princess. She must be dead by now."

"Nope," said Alex. "Not dead. Old. Very old. But not dead."

"How old?"

"Hard to say," I told him. "It's been a bit over three hundred years since she entered the human world, but I don't know how many years she lived before that."

Bennett scowled. "And you've found her?"

Alex smiled. "She's at Happy Oaks!"

"She's my teacher's granny," put in Destiny, who had already heard part of this from Alex and me.

"Ms. Kincaid is willing to help," Alex added.

"Allie, we can't just take an old lady out of the nursing home," said Bennett. He was starting to sound desperate now. "Don't you understand? We'd be arrested! And where am I supposed to take her anyway?"

"To the Enchanted Realm," I said. "It's where she belongs."

"That's it," said Bennett. "I'm out of here. This is just nutty."

When he stood up, Alex said, "You know where else you're going to be out of soon?"

"Where?" he asked, the word coming out almost like a snarl.

"This house. Did you know Dad's company offered to let him keep his job if he came back at the beginning of next week? That's one of the reasons Mom and Dad have been fighting so much. But Dad won't go back as long as the curse is in effect. And you know now that his songs won't ever be any good. So we're going to lose this house if we don't do something and do it fast."

Bennett began walking in a circle, tearing at his hair. My heart went out to the lad. He was past the age of belief, so this was far harder on him than it had been on Alex. (For Destiny, it was no problem at all, of course.)

We waited in silence until he had calmed himself. Finally, still looking furious, he returned to the table.

"Dad's old boss called. He gave Dad until Monday to decide whether to go back to his job," said Alex. "He and mom are going out tomorrow night to discuss it."

"I know they're going out," said Bennett, sounding cranky. "I'm supposed to babysit for you two, remember?"

"So tomorrow night is when we make our move," said

Alex with a smile. Then she reached into my box and took out the piece of wood Granny Squannit had given me. Placing it on the table, she said, "This is a time peg. Before we enter the Enchanted Realm, we pound this into the ground at the point where we plan to go in. It will tie us to that time, so we'll be able to make the trip and return without anyone knowing we've been gone."

"Trip?" Bennett asked. "Don't we just take the old lady in and leave her?"

"Alas, nae," I said. "She must be returned to her mother, the Queen of Shadows. We'll have to cross the sea to do that."

Bennett shook his head. "This is crazy, Al. And not just because this . . . this brownie thing shouldn't even exist. I told you, we can't just take an old lady out of Happy Oaks. It's kidnapping. Or old-lady-napping. And even if we could do that, we'd have to bring her back. Otherwise we'll get arrested for murder or something."

"I believe I can help with that," said a voice from the door.

It was Ms. Kincaid, who had been waiting in the other room.

It was time to hatch our plans.

FROM THE JOURNAL OF
ALEX CARHART

11/6 (Fri.)

I am dizzy with excitement. Tomorrow night we are going to do the most daring and dangerous thing I've ever been a part of. And if all goes well, I am going to get to see the Enchanted Realm!

I can hardly *believe* it.

I just hope nothing goes wrong. If it does, we could end up in prison instead.

Or somehow trapped in the Enchanted Realm.

Mrs. Winterbotham, if you are reading this, don't worry, I'm just making this all up!

On the other hand, if I don't come back, at least you'll know what happened to me. . . .

Saturday, November 7

I write this entry as the children are having a final bicker before we enter the Enchanted Realm. The problem they are discussing is who gets to go.

Bennett is pulling the boy card and saying he should go alone. "Besides," he just said, "if this time peg thing really works, you'll barely know I've been gone. I'll be out and back in an instant."

Which is true enough. However, Alex and Destiny are both insisting they must come as well.

Ailsa McGonagall is snoozing in the portable wheelchair we brought in the boot of Ms. Kincaid's car.

While the children fight, I want to get down what has happened so far this evening. Here it is:

Shortly after Mr. and Mrs. Carhart left for their night out, Lorna Kincaid showed up and we all piled into her car. There was no question about Alex and Destiny coming then, since Bennett was supposed to be "babysitting" (what an odd term to use for children who are nae babes at all) and pretty much forbidden to leave them alone.

When we got to Happy Oaks, Ms. Kincaid parked the car about halfway along the lot, choosing a spot between a couple of bigger cars to help shield us.

"Wait here," she said. "I'll need about twenty minutes."

After she left, Bennett got out of the passenger side, went around the car, and climbed into the driver's seat.

"Are you sure you can do this, Ben?" Alex asked.

He snorted. "If everything you crazies have told me is true, this will be the easiest part of the trip."

To pass the time, I told them more about the Enchanted Realm.

We all knew what was happening inside. Ms. Kincaid was going to sign a permission form that would allow her to take her gran out of the building for some fresh air. The nurse in charge would be warning her that Ailsa was what they call a wanderer, and so she would have to keep a close eye on her.

She would take her gran out, and they would chat for a while. Then, assuming the coast was clear, Lorna would wheel Ailsa over to the car and help her into the front passenger seat.

That accomplished, Bennett would drive us to the nearest church. This was what had Alex so nervous, as I take it the lad is too young to drive in this country. Fortunately, the kirk is no more than a mile away, and it is a quiet country road that leads us there.

Once we were safely away from Happy Oaks, Ms. Kincaid would head back into the nursing home with the empty wheelchair, weeping and wailing about how she had only turned aside to talk to someone for a few minutes and when she turned back, her gran was gone . . .

probably wandered into the woods that surrounded the home.

Happily, that all worked out exactly as we had planned, and Bennett made it to the church with no incident, though I have to say his driving was a bit wombly. At least two times I thought we were headed for the ditch, and for such a short trip, there was a lot of "Oh, God, watch out, Bennett!" from Alex and a lot of "Shut up and let me drive!" back from the lad.

I need to stop now. The fight about who is going into the Realm has been resolved, and it appears we are all going! The nub of it seems to be that Alex was not to be left behind, and if she went, Destiny had to go as well.

Bennett kept insisting that because of the time peg they would not even know he had been gone, but I think none of them are entirely sure the peg will work.

For that matter, neither am I.

Well, there's nothing for it. Bennett is pounding the time peg into the ground. (I give the lad credit for remembering to bring a hammer with him.)

As soon as I put my diary away, I'll be climbing onto Alex's shoulder. Then it's three times widdershins about the kirk for us.

I do not know when I will have the chance to write again.

Date Uncertain (I canna figure how to date this diary entry if we are going to return at the same time we left!)

We have been two days in the Enchanted Realm, but this is the first time I have had a chance to write anything.

To start off, I need to note that we have an unexpected companion. As we were about to go widdershins around the church, Lorna Kincaid came running up, crying, "Wait for me! I've decided to come with you!"

Later, she explained that she had given her report to the nursing home, then dashed off into the woods to "look for her gran"—except, of course, she knew exactly where to find her. She had run all the way to the kirk. I must say she is in extremely good shape for a woman of sixty-five years. I assume that is the elven blood working in her.

So now a party of six—the three Carhart children, the ancient Princess of Sunshine, her great-granddaughter, and myself—went round the church three times.

Because the princess was in a wheelchair and the ground was rough, it took longer than I liked. I was tense with fear that the searchers might have followed Lorna and would come bursting upon us before we finished the third circle. But we made it, and I heard the children gasp as we entered the Enchanted Realm.

It is not that the Realm looks so different at the point where we came through. By sight, it could easily have been their world. But there's no mistaking the Realm for the human world. I can't explain, other than to say you can feel it in your skin. As it turns out, that is literally true for a human, since all three Carharts cried, "It tingles!"

I had not known to expect this, having never brought a human into the Realm before. (And now that I've done it, I quake to think of what price I might pay for the deed. I have violated every point of the Great Oath of the Brownies and then some. I wonder if any brownie has ever before been so bad.)

It was not only the children who cried out. I heard, too, a gasp of delight and pain from Ailsa McGonagall.

"So long," she murmured. "So long away."

Then she stood up from her wheelchair!

"Let me lean on you, Lorna," she said.

"Gladly," replied her great-granddaughter.

We had not been walking more than an hour when Weegun showed up, as I had expected and hoped.

"Well, Angus Cairns," he said, "I keep asking if you have come to steal our lands. Now I find you here with an entire invading party!"

He smiled as he said it, so I knew he had come to help.

I made introductions all around, then said, "Can you take us to the harbor, and the ships you told me of?"

"Yes, and glad to do so," said my friend (for I felt I could now call him that), and off we went.

It was a balmy evening in the Enchanted Realm, unusually warm for November. And a good thing it was, as we did need to stop and sleep for a while. I was worried about the princess lying on the ground, but she said she could feel the Realm seeping into her bones, and it was as good as a tonic for her.

In the morning, I swear she looked younger, though still the crone for all that.

It was good that Alex had prevailed on the matter of joining us, as she was the one who had thought to bring provisions. In fact, her backpack was full of them. Lorna Kincaid was a bit dismayed because the girl had brought nothing but cookies and chips, but the rest of us were pleased enough to have them.

We could smell the sea before we saw it, and despite the terrors of my first trip across, I did like the scent. Soon enough we left the woods and found ourselves atop a hill that sloped down to a sweep of harbor. To my astonishment, there were great docks there, and a dozen graceful ships with sails of silver. Busily moving about the docks were all manner of folk—elves, mostly, but also goblins and dwarves, as well as a small troll. There were also some Makiaweesug.

"Look!" cried Alex, pointing upward. "There's a griffin."

We all looked up, and most of us gasped. It was the first time I had seen one of these great beasts myself, and I marveled at how the eagle's head and wings merged with the lion's body.

"Now I will believe that there are unicorns," murmured Bennett.

For a moment, I thought he had come up with a decent line despite the curse, but then I recognized that he was quoting the great elven poet William Shakespeare. (Most mortals think Shakespeare was a human, but anyone with an ounce of sense can tell he was of Enchanted stock. Half human at most is the general belief in the Enchanted Realm.)

Down to the docks we went, our task to find a ship willing to take us across the Shadow Sea. I had brought my pack and the few coins I had, but I had no idea if they would do for passage.

It turned out they would not, though it took a while to learn that. When we first walked the docks, all we gathered were suspicious looks . . . no surprise, given that I was traveling with such a strange crew of humans, who were nae supposed to be here at all.

For a time it seemed that no one would talk to us. But as I was beginning to despair, a gruff voice shouted, "Destiny! Destiny Carhart, what are you doing here?"

"Herbert!" cried the wee girl happily.

Looking up, I saw a goblin leaning over the edge of a ship. "I'll be right down!" he cried. Moments later, he was standing before us, his ugly face beaming with an enormous grin that showed his pointed teeth.

"Herbert was real?" Bennett cried in astonishment.

Destiny rolled her eyes. "I *told* you he was real, Ben. You just wouldn't believe me. It wasn't very nice of you."

Bennett made an elegant bow. "My apologies, little sister."

By this I saw that even if his poetry itself was atrocious, acting the poet had improved his manners.

I have never had much to do with goblins, but this Herbert seemed nice enough of his type, despite the fact that he was hairless, green, and had great flapping ears.

If I had ears like this, I could fly!

Shoes not needed—goblin feet tougher than leather

Me, being happy I am not a goblin

Angus

He was about three times my height, a few inches shorter than Destiny.

When we explained our problem, Herbert said, "Let me talk to my captain." He turned to the princess. "No offense, ma'am, but I don't think I'll be able to convince the captain to offer free passage, as you hardly look like the Princess of Sunshine. But I can at least get him to talk to you."

A short time later, we were in the captain's quarters. He was a dwarf, about a foot taller than Herbert, with a beard nearly as long as the goblin was high. He was a nice enough fellow, but when I poured out bits o' gold onto his table, he simply laughed.

"Is there naught we can give to convince you to take us across?" I asked.

"Oh, certainly," he said in his rumbling voice. "Give me the hair of the wee lass, which is like to gold, and I'll count it as passage for all of you."

"Oh, captain!" Herbert cried. "That is not right!"

"It's the price," said the captain firmly.

Destiny was starting to cry, but she nodded her assent.

"Wait!" said Alex. "Look."

Swiftly she undid her long braids, revealing the full flood of her bright red hair, which was like a fire ablaze.

The captain studied her for a long moment, then nodded and said, "Aye, that will do."

Oh, my heart went out to my girl then. I knew how she loved those braids, and that bright red hair.

"Herbert, go fetch the scissor man," said the captain.

Then we sat and waited.

"Alex?" said Bennett.

"Shhhh," she said, her face set. "We have to do what we have to do."

Moments later, the scissor man came and said, "'Twill be easier if you braid it back up, miss."

This she did, her fingers moving fast. And when she was done, she sat silently weeping while he took his great scissors and chopped off first the left braid, then the right, laying each across the captain's table.

"Passage paid," said the captain. "Your timing is good. We sail within the hour."

FROM THE JOURNAL OF
ALEX CARHART

First Day on Ship

I cried myself to sleep last night. I still can't believe I let the scissor man cut off my braids. It's strange that something that didn't hurt at all (I mean, there's no pain when you cut hair) could hurt so very much, so deep inside.

I keep putting my hands to my head, feeling that short shag of hair.

Each time I do, it feels wrong.

I don't even want to think what Mom and Dad are going to say when we get back.

Assuming we do get back.

Despite all this, I am starting to think maybe it was worth it. Seriously, I keep pinching myself to make sure I'm not dreaming and we truly are crossing the Shadow Sea on a silver ship with a crew of elves and goblins! (The goblins are a riot. There are five of them, each about three feet tall. They have big noses, big feet, flapping ears, and think farts are the most hilarious things in the world.)

Last night I saw a mermaid swimming beside us. She waved to me, then flipped up her tail, laughed, and dove out of sight.

I had to hug myself to keep from exploding!

Poor Bennett is not having nearly as good a time. That's because the curse is still in effect and he's trying to write poems that capture (in his words) "the wonder and glory and awe of this voyage."

Naturally, they suck.

At least it's not his fault. But even knowing that, he can't help trying. I never would have believed I could feel so sorry for him. The best thing he's come up with so far is a quick two-liner to disapprove of how much the goblins fart:

Upon my soul, I think it crass
The way these goblins pass their gas!

Actually, it's probably the best poem he's written.

In other news, the princess is looking younger by the hour. Even now, when she still looks kind of old, you can see how incredibly beautiful she must have been when Ewan first met her. No wonder he fell in love with her.

I wonder exactly how Ewan is related to us. Super-great-uncle? Many times great-granddaddy? It would be cool to find out. Maybe I'll have to learn how to do a family tree when we get back. I'll definitely need the "intermagoogle" to research our family.

Destiny is so happy to have Herbert to play with again. The captain has had to yell at them twice because Herbert has been neglecting his work to play tag with my little sister.

It turns out that the reason he had been her not-so-imaginary friend was that he had a few weeks of shore leave.

The world is turning out to be far stranger than I had realized.

Fourth Day Since Entering the Enchanted Realm

The captain and I spent the better part of the afternoon trying to coach Bennett in how to present the Princess of Sunshine to her mother once we reach the queen's court.

(Ailsa has been youthening, and now that the captain has realized who his passenger really is, he canna do enough for us.)

The lad is respectful enough and is trying hard. But due to the curse, he is unable to control his poetic urge and launches into cascades of words that strain to sound lofty and graceful but just seem idiotic.

'Tis a hard and harsh curse indeed.

Though the journey has been mostly peaceful, we did have some unwelcome excitement last night when we crossed ways with a sea serpent. The scaly thing reared out of the water and was going to wrap itself around the ship. Surely it would have dragged us to the bottom of the Shadow Sea if it had been able to do so.

As it turns out, this is why the captain keeps goblins on the crew. The five of them sprang into action and attacked the monster with their bare hands! I never thought I would live to see a goblin perched on the head of a sea serpent and pummeling it between the eyes.

It was over soon enough, but I was glad Destiny was

already asleep, for she would have been terrified about what might happen to Herbert. As it was, the crew had to fish the poor fellow out of the water.

This is not the life for a brownie! I am supposed to be inside, keeping things tidy, not having an adventure!

FROM THE JOURNAL OF ALEX CARHART

Third Day on Ship

Here is something I will never forget. A little while ago I was on deck. The princess is almost fully herself now, and so beautiful it almost hurts my eyes to look at her. The crew found a dress for her somewhere. It's not much, but better than the flannel nightgown she had been wearing.

Anyway, she was standing at the prow of the ship, her golden hair streaming in the wind. The four of us—me and Bennett and Destiny, and Angus on my shoulder—came up behind her.

Ms. Kincaid joined us.

Ailsa turned and smiled, and I saw then why she was called the Princess of Sunshine, for it was as if in that moment a new sun had risen just for us.

Ahead I could see the harbor, with a flock of elven ships.

Beyond them rose a hill, and at the top of it was a soaring silver palace.

I get a chill just writing about it.

CONNECTICUT COAST TOWN CRIER

NEW GLASGOW, CT

MYSTERIOUS DISAPPEARANCE AT HAPPY OAKS

by Emily Goldstein

There was a disturbing incident at the Happy Oaks Senior Home last Saturday night. At about 7:30 p.m., Ms. Lorna Kincaid came in to take her great-grandmother, Mrs. Ailsa McGonagall, "out for some air." Some twenty minutes later, Kincaid returned to the lobby, frantic because her great-grandmother, who was noted in the home's records as a "wanderer," had disappeared while Kincaid was talking with someone else.

A search was mounted, but no sign of the old woman was found.

Even more mysterious, Ms. Kincaid has vanished as well. Her car was found in the parking lot of the First Baptist Church, and there are footprints and wheelchair tracks going around the church. But there has been no sign of the two women. Neither is there any sign of a struggle or of foul play.

The police are mystified by the situation. The nursing home will not give a further statement at this time.

Anyone with information regarding the fate of the two women is urged to contact the New Glasgow Police Station.

By the time we reached the eastern shore of the Shadow Sea, the princess was as herself as she could be, and the crew of the ship was entirely at her service. Never have I heard so many apologies. I could see fear in many of those faces, elf and dwarf and goblin alike, as they wondered what the queen might do when she learned they had nearly denied her daughter passage.

His face grim, the captain offered to return Alex's braids. She looked at them, a pair of fine red ropes lying limp across his outstretched hands, and just shook her head.

From a perch atop the mainmast, a signal elf had sent word to shore of the precious and amazing cargo we were carrying into harbor. So it was no surprise that there was a great crowd gathered at the pier.

At the center of the crowd were the queen's guards, tall elves in silvery mail, holding back the masses. The guards had a grand cart, drawn by four white horses, into which we were guided. I clung tight to Alex's shoulder, fearing to fall and be trampled by the crowd, as tall to me as trees would be to a human.

Up the hill we rode, cheering throngs on either side, until we reached the gate of the castle.

There stood the queen herself, robed all in black, with her midnight hair flowing past her shoulders in thick ebony curls. About her neck hung the great ruby. In her arms she carried a robe of glistening white.

For a moment, no one moved. Then I poked Alex. She got the message and poked Bennett. "You're on!" she hissed.

Beautiful!

The Queen of Shadows

But terrifying!

Angus

Bennett swallowed hard, then stepped down from the cart. As we had taught him, he made a deep bow. Then he straightened and said, "Oh, most queenly queen of queenliness."

I groaned inside. On the other hand, the queen could hardly fault him for this, since it was her own curse at work.

I saw one corner of her mouth twitch.

"I, Bennett Carhart, male of the McGonagall line, have the fruitful honor and luminescent privilege to return to you your long-lost daughter, the Princess of Sunshine."

The boy was sweating and looked like he was about to faint, but I thought he had done well, given the circumstances and the curse.

On cue, the princess stepped from the cart.

The queen stared at her, then murmured, "Long have you been gone, my child."

"Longer than I intended," replied the princess, "and a strange time it has been."

"Would you do it again?" asked the queen.

"Aye, for love, I would do it again."

The queen's eyes flashed. For a terrible moment, I thought I saw a fury rising in her and feared she would once more banish the girl. But she took a deep breath, then nodded and said, "Well, then I guess you made the right choice after all."

Seventh Day of Our Journey

An unexpected turn, and a dark time for me. I didn't see it coming, for last night started delightfully. The queen declared a grand feast, a celebration with wonders and fireworks and food beyond any I had ever imagined: jellies condensed from dew that was harvested from butterfly wings just before dawn; bread made from the crushed seeds of roses and eglantine, so soft and light it was in danger of floating away; mushroom tarts that glowed in the dark; and many, many more strange and luscious things.

Ailsa came to us before the banquet began to assure us it would be safe for the Carhart children to eat the food, and that it would not be used to hold them here.

To my fear and delight, we were seated at the queen's table. There was a special chair for me, with a kind of small table all my own, so that I could be up with the others.

The laughter, and the songs, and the celebration, and the elf wine, which I drank a bit more of than I should have . . . oh, 'twas a wondrous night.

Just as the merriment was reaching its peak, the queen went to her throne and called for the Carharts to present themselves before her.

They stood in line by age. The queen rose and went down to them, stopping first before Bennett. Placing her slender hand upon his shoulder, she said, "And so a male of the McGonagall line has returned to me what a male of that same line took away. And for that deed, I declare the Curse of the McGonagalls to be lifted."

Bennett, bless him, had the good sense to bow. As he did, the queen placed her hands upon his head and murmured, "For what you have done, I grant you, Bennett Carhart, the gift of song."

When he stood again, I would have sworn that he was glowing.

Then to Alex she gave a slender ring, saying, "With this ring, you will always know when someone is speaking true, and thus no boy nor man can play you false."

I expect she will find that very useful as she grows a bit older.

"And you, wee Destiny," she said to the youngest Carhart. "What can I give to you, who became part of my daughter's destiny?"

The girl thought for a moment, then said, "Can Herbert the Goblin come back to visit whenever he wants?"

The queen laughed. "Not whenever he wants, my child. But he may make three trips a year. And with this amulet I now give you, you may three times summon him if ever you are in danger. But use it wisely, for it is three times and three times only."

Next she called Lorna Kincaid to stand before her.

"And so you are of my blood," said the queen, gazing at her. "A great-great-granddaughter. And you helped to restore my daughter to me. For this I owe you much. Tell me, descendant mine, what is your wish . . . to stay here in the Realm, or return to the world you were raised in?"

"May I stay?" asked Lorna.

The queen nodded. "You may stay as long as you like," she said, "and return when you wish, if ever that time may arise. For you have done me great service."

Then the queen called for me to come and stand before her.

I was giddy with delight, sure that I, too, was about to receive my reward. So I was shocked at what she said next.

"Angus Cairns. Angus Cairns. What are we to do with you? You have done me great service, great service indeed. But in doing so, you have broken every part of the Great Oath of the Brownies to which you swore long ago."

I hung my head and murmured, "Aye, that I have."

"Were it up to me, I would blink at these transgressions and pretend they never happened. But we are ruled by laws and bindings, as well you know. So I must hold you here until we can summon the tribunal and determine exactly what is to be done with you."

"No!" cried Alex.

Oh, the sound of that "No!" was balm to my heart. Naetheless, I wish I could have stopped it in her mouth. One does not lightly cry "No!" to the Queen of Shadows!

The queen turned, her eyes blazing. Then she closed them. I saw her lips moving, and realized that she was counting.

After a moment or two, she opened her eyes and said, "Because you are human and do not know our ways, I will forgive that outburst. But do not ever speak to me in such a way again if you value your life or your chance of return to the human world."

Then she gathered her robes about her and left the banquet hall, which had fallen silent.

Soon two elves approached the Carharts and said, "We will guide you to your rooms. Tomorrow you take ship for home."

Then two goblins crossed to me and said sternly, "Come with us, Angus Cairns. You will be housed in comfort and ease, but no more about shall you go until the tribunal passes judgment."

"Angus!" cried Alex. She stretched towards me, but the elves pulled her back, a sight that still burns in my memory.

I drew this because I could not stop thinking about it.

"Travel safe, all three!" I cried. I tried to move to her, but the goblins grabbed me by the shoulders and marched me away, and I saw the Carharts no more.

I would say this is not the way I thought this would end, but I have long dreaded that the day would come when I would pay for breaking the Great Oath so many times over. And here it is at last.

I hope the time peg works for the children. It torments me that I am not able to be with them on their homeward trip.

FROM THE JOURNAL OF ALEX CARHART

11/7 (Sat.)

The time peg worked!

It was amazing—I had lost track of how many days we were in the Enchanted Realm, but last night we came back into the human world (as I now know it is called) at exactly the same time we left. (I checked the clock in Ms. Kincaid's car.)

We didn't dare have Bennett drive the car back to our place, of course, so we had to walk. Ben had to carry Destiny about half the way, but he never complained about it.

I could do worse in terms of a big brother.

Mom got called back to Happy Oaks because of Ailsa's disappearance, so it wasn't till morning that she saw what had happened to my hair.

I won't write down the scene that followed. It was too unpleasant. What was really unfair was that she grounded Bennett for letting me do it!

Poor Ben. Now that the curse is off, he just wants to get back to soccer. It's going to be a while before that can happen. I feel really bad for him. But we had a talk about it, and he said that he'd trade a couple of weeks of grounding for an adventure like the one we just had any time he got the chance.

I eavesdropped on Mom and Dad talking this afternoon. I think Dad is going to ask for his job back!

If only I wasn't so worried about Angus, everything would be great....

From the desk of
SHEILA WINTERBOTHAM

Friday, November 13

Dear Mr. and Mrs. Carhart—

I wanted to take a moment to tell you that I am impressed by the progress Alex has made. Though her desk is not likely to win any awards for organization and neatness, it does now qualify as civilized. More important, she has started to get her work in on time.

I don't know what you have done to achieve this metamorphosis, but I salute you for it. Maybe you should consider teaching a training class for parents.

Sincerely,
Sheila Winterbotham

FROM THE JOURNAL OF
ALEX CARHART

11/14 (Sat.)

It's been a week since we left Angus and Ms. Kincaid in the Enchanted Realm, and my room is getting to be a mess again.

I'm honestly trying to keep it neater. Partly because I know that's what Angus would want.

Really, it just seems so strange not to have him here. Yeah, he drove me nuts when he first showed up. But by the time we went to the Enchanted Realm, I had really come to like him.

Now I miss the little guy like crazy.

I suppose I should put the Barbie dollhouse (the Pink Horror!) back in the attic. The thing is, I keep hoping he'll come back, if only for a visit.

Okay, that's probably stupid of me. But I'm so worried about him! He did such a great thing in returning the princess to the Enchanted Realm, and look what he got for it.

The Realm may be beautiful, but I don't think it is always fair.

On the plus side, things are much better here. Dad has gone back to work, and Bennett is his normal annoying self again. Except he sings a lot now, and it's really beautiful. So that's cool. Also, Dad has made up with Pete and has agreed to stick to writing music and let Pete handle the lyrics. They've decided to record some of their new songs with Bennett singing them.

Best of all, Mom and Dad are getting along.

I'm even doing better in school, mostly thanks to the way Angus helped me get organized.

It's just not fair that the queen is going to put him on trial for breaking some stupid Oath of the Brownies! He was doing good things. Shoot, I'm crying again.

Talk about stupid!

The Judgment Upon Angus Cairns as Declared by the High Court of the Enchanted Realm in Scotland

After due consideration of the numerous violations of the Great Oath of the Brownies that have been perpetrated by Angus Cairns in a remarkably short period of time, the court has come to its decision, which is as follows:

First and foremost, as a result of these many violations, Angus Cairns is now and forevermore to be branded a rascal. Henceforth, his full and formal name shall be Angus Cairns (Rascal).

Second, though the curse laid upon his line as a result of his interfering father Seamus Cairns (Rascal) has now been lifted, it is ruled that for his many violations of the Great Oath of the Brownies, including insufficient mischief, being seen by humans, and worst of all, bringing humans into the Enchanted Realm, Angus Cairns (Rascal) shall be sentenced to serve additional time with the family to which he is now attached.

The court was in favor of an additional fifty years. However, the queen in her mercy has declared that in exchange for his role in returning the Princess of Sunshine to the Enchanted Realm, this term shall be reduced to five years, at which time Angus Cairns (Rascal) will be free to attach himself to any family he wishes.

So it is decreed, and so shall it be.

KINDERGARTEN!

November 18

Dear Parents:

My name is Jill Dietz, and I am delighted that I will be working with your kindergartners for the rest of the year. One of my primary responsibilities over the next few months will be helping your children to cope with the unusual disappearance of Ms. Kincaid. With that in mind, I want to invite you to contact me at any time if you have concerns about your child and his or her progress, or how she or he is dealing with this transition.

I will do all I can to make this a wonderful year of growth and learning for your child.

Sincerely,
Jill Dietz

Dear Mr. and Mrs. Carhart—

I wanted to let you know that of all the children in the class, Destiny is the one who is best dealing with this situation. She is a calm and happy child. On the other hand, I do have some concerns about her clearly overactive imagination. Someday we need to have a conversation about Herbert the Goblin.

All best,
Jill Dietz

Saturday, November 21

I am back with the Carharts! Of the journey home there is not much to say. As I was sentenced to return here by the High Court, my passage was paid. The ship was smooth and fast, and I had a good time playing knucklebones with Herbert the Goblin. We swapped stories about the Carharts, and he has promised to come visit the next time he has leave. I know this will make Destiny happy.

I did—as I was bound to do, and would have been a fool not to do—take a bit of a detour to tell Granny Squannit all that had happened. She pronounced herself well pleased, and with that blessing, I headed for home.

I reached the house late at night, and when I went through the flap I found Bubbles at his bowl in the kitchen.

"You're back!" he said in surprise.

"Aye, that I am," I replied.

"That's good," he said. "I've missed you."

I recounted for him some of our adventures, and promised to tell the rest on the morrow. "But right now," I said, "I am fiercely tired and need to sleep."

I was in the Pink Horror when Alex woke.

I found myself in the mood for a bit of mischief. (After all, the court itself had declared I had been lax in this department!) So when I came out of the house and she cried, "You've come back!" I did not tell her right away of my sentence.

This was also partly because I was not sure how she felt about my return. So I experienced a happy warmth in my heart when she said, "I've been so worried about you, Angus! How did you make out in your trial?"

"Well, the sentence was a bit harsh. . . ."

"That's not fair! You did a great thing by bringing the princess back to her mother."

"Oh, aye. But I hardly did it on my own. And I broke many a rule in the doing of it."

Alex said nothing for a bit. Finally she said, in a voice not like herself, "So do you have to go?"

"Nae, but I do not want to stay where I am not wanted."

Which was true, if not the entire story.

"Well, who says I don't want you?" she asked indignantly.

"You did, many and many a time."

"Well, you don't always believe everything I say, do you?"

Still in the mood for a wee bit o' mischief, I told a wee bit of a lie. "Well, I canna stay without you asking me."

She rolled her eyes, put her hands on her hips, then looked at me straight and said, "Angus Cairns, will you stay? You need a home, and I need a brownie."

Trying to keep the tears from my eyes—really, I'm

getting far too sentimental as I grow older—I said, "Alex Carhart, I would be glad to stay and be your brownie true."

"Let's swear on it," she said.

Then she licked her thumb and held it out.

I licked mine and did the same.

We pressed them together, and thus it was settled and sealed.

I expect that many a day the girl is going to drive me stark-raving mad.

I plan to do my best to return the favor.

But oh and och, 'tis good to have a home again.

Every brownie needs one.

AUTHOR'S NOTE
(with interruptions)

Dear Reader—

...writer has to do what a writer has to do. And when a cranky brownie shows up in a writer's office with a stack of papers and says, "Here, take a look at this." A writer with any sense had best pay attention.

...you know by now ... and say "brownie." I am not ... thing about a small girl in a tan uniform who might want to sell me Thin Mint cookies.

I am talking about a genuine Scottish brownie: a household spirit just shy of twelve inches, able to appear and disappear in mysterious ways, obsessively tidy, and given to ... well ... bouts of temper.

But rather than going on about this, I think it be better for me to let Angus Og ... speak for himself.

AUTHOR'S NOTE
(with interruptions)

Dear Reader—

A writer has to do what a writer has to do. And when a cranky brownie shows up in a writer's office with a stack of papers and says, "Here, take a look at this!" a writer with any sense had best pay attention.

As you know by now, when I say "brownie," I am not talking about a small girl in a tan uniform who might want to sell me Thin Mint cookies.

I am talking about a genuine Scottish brownie, a household spirit just shy of twelve inches, able to appear and disappear in mysterious ways, obsessively tidy, and given to, well . . . bouts of temper.

But rather than going on about this, I think it's best for me to let Angus Cairns speak for himself. . . .

✦　✦　✦

Dear Reader—

I hope you'll forgive the rather rude lead-in to my message to you. You would think a writer would ha' more discretion than that! On the other hand, what can you expect of someone who is only two-thirds of the way to his hundredth birthday? The man is still wet behind the ears!

Anyway, the Coville has asked me to give you a few words about what you have just read, which is my own diary, torn from the deepest part of my heart.

First off, I don't know that it was necessary for him to stick in all those other things (the stuff he calls "documents"). I was perfectly happy with what I had written.

He claims that everyone needs to be edited.

I claim that everything was already neat and tidy before he started mucking about with it.

He claims that "editing" is not just tidying up.

Ah weel, I suppose he's the expert. And what's done is done. So right now, I just wanted to thank you for reading my story, which is absolutely true.

If you like it, please share it with your friends.

If you don't, then please keep your festerin' gob shut and don't embarrass yourself by displaying your lack of taste!

Sincerely,

Angus Cairns

✦ ✦ ✦

Dear Reader—

Please excuse that last outburst from Angus. I leave it in only to give you a sense of what I have had to deal with while helping him shape his story into a book. I only put up with his outbursts because he had such a compelling story to tell. Well, to be completely honest, there is also the fact that despite his bursts of temper, the little fellow can be quite endearing.

Anyway, I hope your enjoyment in reading his tale will be proportionate to the distress I suffered in getting it out of him!

With many thanks,
Bruce Coville

✦ ✦ ✦

Dear Reader,

I am writing this at midnight, in order that I might have some privacy. I can do this because I have learned how to turn on the Coville's "laptop" (which seems an odd name for the thing, as it sits on his desk most of the time).

Let me start by saying that typing is not easy for me. That is partly because I have never used one of these wretched devices before. But the bigger problem is that I have to hunt all over the "keyboard" to find the letters. Why? Because they are all scrambled up!

I ask you, what in the world were the people who

made this machine thinking? Why would they start with QWERTY as the first six letters? Is there something wrong with the alphabet in this country?

I swear, the things a brownie has to put up with!

Anyway, the third thing that makes this difficult is that, due to my size, I have to lean over at the waist and stretch my arms to hit most letters ... which I must do with my fist, my hands being so small.

So this is taking me a fair bit o' time to write.

The reason I'm bothering is that I wanted to warn you that you shouldna pay too much attention to anything the Coville says. I have checked out his writings, and all he does is make stuff up! So if he tells you I have displayed ill temper or been difficult to work with, just remember that this is a man who makes his living by telling lies to children!

'Tis a shameful business, if you ask me.

—Angus Cairns

✦ ✦ ✦

Dear Reader—

Though I am fond of Angus in general, I must admit that I will be somewhat relieved when we have finished our revision work (only a day or two to go!) and he can return to his regular job of a/n/n/o/y/i/n/g/ /A/l/e/x/ /C/a/r/ . . . keeping Alex Carhart's room clean.

—Bruce Coville

✦   ✦   ✦

Dear Reader—

The man is unbelievable!

All I did was offer him some haggis. . . .

—AC

✦   ✦   ✦

Dear Angus—

I am sorry I turned down your offer of a sheep's stomach stuffed with oatmeal and chopped-up sheep's heart, liver, and lungs. That was culturally insensitive of me.

—BC

✦   ✦   ✦

BC—

Apology accepted. But did you see what showed up at the door last night? I decided that this would be the best time to depart. I will wait for you to send copies of our book when it is published. Thank you for your help, even the part that was annoying.

—AC

✦   ✦   ✦

Dear Reader—

I am sorry Angus left without saying good-bye. Despite his prickliness, I had been enjoying his company.

Anyway, I have my hands full with another project now. It appears that word has spread in the Enchanted Realm that I am the go-to guy for a creature (or "being," as I have been informed) that wants to share its diary.

I wasn't entirely surprised by that. Word of these things does get around.

Even so, I wasn't expecting what I discovered when I opened the back door this morning.

It was a griffin!

I leaped backward, my heart pounding in terror. I mean, the creature was big enough to bite my head off! Fortunately, that was not what he had in mind. And when I realized that he had a human boy standing next to him, I calmed down a bit.

Their names are Gerald Overflight (the griffin) and Bradley Ashango (the boy). And boy, do they have a story to tell!

I can't wait to share it with you.

—BC

Turn the page for a sneak peek at

"Bruce Coville is a WIZARD at telling stories."
—Christopher Paolini, *New York Times* bestselling author of *Eragon*

The Enchanted Files

HATCHED

Bruce Coville
Bestselling author of *My Teacher Is an Alien*

Coming October 2016

Gentle Reader—

I am pleased, but nervous, to present this account of my adventures in the human world and what happened to me there.

To give you the story completely, I have woven into my diary (which was originally intended to be quite personal!) many documents and papers that I hope will help you fully understand the terror and the drama of it all.

Gaaah! That sounds a little over the top, doesn't it? Well, my teacher, Master Abelard (whom you will meet later in these pages), has occasionally called me a drama queen.

I will not demean myself by explaining what that means, but I sometimes fear it is true.

On the other wing, I did indeed experience a great deal of terror on this journey. So that is also true.

In addition to my diary, you will find many pages from the journal of a human boy named Bradley Ashango, as well as photographs he took with a strange device called a cell phone. He swears the thing is not magical, merely scientific. I am not entirely convinced of this. It certainly seems magical to me.

Many times Brad and I had written about the same

experience, so I trimmed some of our entries to avoid unnecessary repetition. However, nothing has been added! We want you to experience this as we did.

Well, not *entirely* as we did. I suffered a great deal of fear, doubt, and emotional agony during the events here recounted. Though I hope you will read with a sympathetic heart, I also hope that the emotional effects will not be as overwhelming for you while reading it as they were for me while living it.

One last note: Please excuse my poetry. Master Abelard tells me it is not very good. But it is part of who I am, so I felt it was important to leave it in place.

Yours very sincerely,
Gerald Overflight, Griffin

The Code of the Griffins

I. A griffin is brave and fierce in all situations. The heart quails not, and the beak and talons are ever ready to strike in the name of truth and freedom.

II. Now that Great Alexander has left the human world, and the divine Dante has gone to the Fields of the Blessed, griffins are no more to be seen by humans.

III. We are guardians of treasure, and any item of value placed in a griffin's care, whether it be glittering diamond or hope of heaven, will be protected unto the death. A griffin who fails in this regard is no griffin at all.

IV. The Enchanted Realm is our home and haven, and we go no more to the human world.

V. We live in a state of joy and gratitude that we have been given the gift of the sky. And we are ever thankful for these treasures: the power of wings, the ferocity of heart, the strength of limb, and the purity of intent that make us, now and evermore . . . GRIFFINS!

This is the Code of the Griffins, as given to us by Izzikiah Wildbeak and written down by Josiah Cloudclaws in *The Griffinagria*.

Reader—

I put in the Code so you would understand the kind of pressure I was facing. We grifflings ("grifflings" is the word for young griffins) are given a copy of this document on our seventh Hatchday and ordered to memorize it. Our elders expect that within two weeks we will be able to recite word for word any item on the list when asked.

Now that you've seen the Code, it's time to show you my actual diary, which starts on the next page. You will always be able to tell when it's me writing, because I begin my entries with the full day and date. (Brad claims this is overly fussy, but I think it's the proper way to do it.)

For ease of reading, I have converted the dates of events in the Enchanted Realm to match corresponding days in the human world.

You're welcome.

—G.O.

Friday, June 19

This was a bad day, mostly due to the continued teasing from my rotten siblings, who claim I am not a true griffin.

This wounds me.

In fact, today it made me so mad that I wrote a poem about Cyril:

Higgledy-piggledy,
Berries and tarts,
Cyril's the king
Of huge stinky farts!

That made me feel better.

I'm going to try to write a poem every day. They seem to help me get my feelings out.

To check the claims of the SS (Stupid Siblings) that I am not a true griffin, I looked up "griffins" in our family's copy of the *Encyclopedia Enchantica*.

Having read what the *EE* has to say, my response is "What a lot of unicorn poop!"

Encyclopedia Enchantica

GRIFFINS

The griffin is a creature of enormous power, blessed with the head and wings of an eagle and the hindquarters of a lion. The upper part of the front legs is also lionlike. However, they taper down to become more birdlike, finally ending in the fierce talons of an eagle.

The only exception to the eagle/lion mix is the griffin's ears, which are long and horselike, though they thrust out sideways rather than standing straight up as a horse's do. This adds an oddly comic touch to the griffin's otherwise dignified and ferocious appearance.

As the eagle is the lord of all birds and the lion the king of beasts, the griffin, which combines the two forms, is considered the monarch of all creatures.

Griffins (also known as "griffons" or "gryphons," but here we use the preferred spelling) are often guardians of treasure. They have a deep and abiding love for gold, jewels, and all manner of precious things.

They also guard reputation, a different kind of treasure, one that is uniquely valuable.

A griffin's claw is said to have medicinal properties, and a feather from its wings is supposedly able to restore sight to the blind. (It is not clear whether the latter is actually true.)

Because of its mix of parts, the griffin is seen as having a dual nature. For some it is a symbol of the divine. For others it is ferocity on the wing, the very sight of which terrorizes all but the bravest of men.

Indeed, the griffin community divided over these very matters in the Great Griffin Schism of 1792, which led to the establishment of the American Aerie.

Heloise Batwing, Dwarf
Lead Scholar, Guild Hall

All right, I'll admit the encyclopedia describes what I *look like* well enough, right down to my ears.

But that whole thing about being ferocious?

HAH! And again, HAH!

Okay, I suppose a lot of griffins really are ferocious.

Okay, maybe *most* griffins are ferocious.

Unfortunately, I don't qualify. Except, of course, when I get really angry. But that never lasts for long and usually ends in tears.

Mine.

Good grief! Does what I just wrote mean that my rotten siblings are right when they say I'm not a true griffin? Great Izzikiah, maybe it's so. Right now I do not feel ferocious.

Mostly what I feel is frettingly nervous.

I'd write a poem about it, but I've already done one for today.

The reason I am nervous is simple: In only twenty-four days, my Tenth Hatchday (which is supposed to be a major holiday) will arrive. Alas, this is not my real Hatchday, simply the one we *count* as my Hatchday, for reasons I would rather not discuss.

The problem is, I must acquire a True Treasure by

then or be declared not a True Griffin . . . this time not by my sibs but by Artoremus Lashtail, the High Lord of the Griffin Stronghold of the Northern Quarter. And it will happen in front of everyone we know, at the Hatchday Gathering at the Great Cavern.

I cannot bear to think of Father's disappointment if I do not succeed in this. But I have no idea what to get or where to get it. I have been fretting about this, but I have not been *thinking* about it as I should. This is because treasure does not interest me as much as it is supposed to.

I really am a very bad griffin.

The situation is so awful that I am seriously considering running away!

But where? Pretty much anywhere I go in the Enchanted Realm, they would find me. That leaves only the human world.

But that idea is too horrible to even consider!

June 20

Dear Mom,

I'm writing to ask if Brad can stay with you again this summer. He had a great time last year, and right now Manhattan looks to be even hotter than it was then. (Global warming . . . a topic on which we actually agree!)

To be honest, it's not just the heat. It's been a bad year for Brad. He's had to deal with a fair amount of bullying at school. Not as bad as at the old school, but even so . . .

Also, he's really been missing his dad. It's been almost two years, but sometimes I think it's even worse for him now than it was when it happened. Maybe it's just that the older a boy gets, the more he needs to have his dad around. Or at least some man in his life. So I'm thinking maybe your buddy Herb will be good for him.

Look, Mom, I know the two of us still aren't getting along that well. But Brad loves his "Bibi," and I think this would be really good for him.

What do you say?

Love,
Delia

Sunday, June 21

Sometimes I wish I were an only child!
Seriously.
It's not that I don't love my sibs.
Well, in a way.
If I really, really try . . .

Boogers and gumballs,
A shred and a shard,
Loving my siblings
Is pretty darn hard!

This love thing is a mystery, and the kind of question my teacher, Master Abelard, likes to discuss. Should you have to *try* to love someone? Shouldn't it come naturally?

He can talk about that kind of thing for hours.

Love or not, natural or not, I can't take Cyril's bossiness and Violet's snippiness any longer.

It didn't help that Violet had her Pegasus friend Aerilinn over today. The two of them are so snotty when they're together! (And it is well known that there is nothing snottier than a snotty Pegasus!) I wish I had never accepted the feather from Aerilinn's right wing that

Violet gave me on our eighth Hatchday. It truly is a thing of beauty and a fine treasure. But it wasn't worth what I've had to put up with from the two of them ever since.

What I wish even more is that Mom hadn't slipped last month and told my brat brother and snippy sister the true story of our Hatchday.

Days.

I know Mom regrets this now that she sees how they use it against me (though she only sees a small part of it). But there's no taking it back, and ever since it came out, my sibs have been so full of themselves it makes me want to yark up a hair ball.

Which just shows how annoying they are, since I *hate* puking up hair balls. It is impossible to have any sense of dignity while you are doing it! Okay, I know. Cats of all sizes cough up hair balls all the time. But even though I have the body of a lion, having the head of an eagle makes spitting up those wretched, soggy globs of fur truly disgusting. I especially hate it when they get caught on my beak and dangle there like giant juicy boogers!

Stupid hair balls.

Oh well. At least I have talons in front and claws in back. That is kind of cool, since it makes me extremely dangerous.

Yes! That is me! Gerald the Invincible!

Blarg.

I am about as invincible as a daisy.

Anyway, between Violet and Aerilinn teasing me this morning, and that wing whap Cyril landed on the back of my head this afternoon, today was the last straw. I have decided for sure. I am going to run away to the human world.

Yes, the human world!

I can just imagine Violet gasping in horror and telling me this will be a violation of the Code of the Griffins. Which is actually true. But how griffinlike is it for them to pick on me the way they do? Don't they have any sense of family honor?

I can also imagine Cyril (or, more technically, Cyril-the-Pain) correcting me to point out that a griffin would not "run away"; he would "*fly* away." He is so literal-minded! It makes it useless, but kind of funny, to make puns at him. For example, if I tried to point out that Fly Away would make a good name for an insect repellent, he would never get it.

I like making puns. Alas, Master Abelard claims it is a bad habit and not something I should indulge in.

Well, pun or not, bad habit or not, I *am* going to fly away!

Once I am free of my brat brother and snippy sister, and no longer under my parents' wings (so to speak), I can start developing my own true life.

If only the idea weren't so scary!

But if I don't do this, I'll be a griffin wuss forever!